THE REAPER AND HIS ANGEL

FORBIDDEN SERIES: BOOK ONE

DANI RENÉ

DEDICATION

To the kick ass women who love delving into something darker and aren't afraid to admit it. I hope you find a new best friend in Angel.

To the babes who love a man that can be an asshole, but also loves fiercely. I hope you all find a new book boyfriend in Samael.

Before you start, know that this isn't a fairytale.

This isn't a story filled with roses, rainbows, and sunshine. It's raw, emotionally draining, and it's brutal. It will be difficult to read, and there are parts you might not agree with, or even enjoy. That's okay. That's exactly what I wanted from this story.

I didn't plan on it. The characters came to me and told me their story. They consumed me daily until I wrote the last word. I hope they capture you as they have me.
As many dark parts as there are in Sam and Angel's journey, there is light as well.

Does the dark prince save the day?
Or does his princess have to say goodbye?

You'll just have to read it and see.

PLAYLIST

The Weekend - Angel
Breaking Benjamin - Dance With The Devil
The Weekend - In The Night
The Weekend - Pretty
Bullet For My Valentine - Venom
Bullet For My Valentine - Dirty Little Secret
Seether - Broken
HIM - Don't Fear The Reaper
Aaron Richards - Monster
Lo-Fang - You're The One That I Want
Breaking Benjamin - Angels Fall

For the full playlist, head to my Spotify

Crave

Verb [used with object]
Feel a powerful desire for (something)

PROLOGUE
Samael

I stalk into the hallway with my mind on everything but work. I need to get out of this house. I need a fucking break, but Father has kept me here training the girls. He instructs me to be brutal, which I am. As much as I enjoy it, though, I don't want to do it anymore.

There's been an influx of girls, and I'm exhausted.

What man in their right mind can say they're tired of fucking? Well, I am.

Pulling the tie from around my neck, I wrap it tight around my hand and undo the top two buttons of my gray dress shirt. The meeting with daddy dearest went as expected, like shit. Ever since my brother got banished from the mansion over a year ago, and I managed to help that feisty little thing escape two months ago, he's been in a mood.

It's as if a fucking hurricane hit, sending us all into turmoil, and I'm the one left to pick up the debris.

My father—Harlan Wolfe—is a destructive force when he's in a good mood. But this fuck up that my brother caused has put him in one of the worst moods ever.

When I reach the room he sent me to, I find a beautiful little chocolate-haired beauty sitting on the perfectly made up bed. "And you are?" I growl. My voice echoes in the empty room, and I see her shudder in response. It's beautiful when they're scared. Makes them taste that much sweeter.

"Amy." She has the sweetest, most melodic voice I've ever heard. I stare at her for a moment too long. Her face is a picture of hope, but that's not what she should be looking at me with. No. She should be staring at me with fear.

"Kneel." Automatically, she drops to her knees, and my mouth curls into a satisfied smirk.

Good girl.

Those are the words I should praise her with, but I don't. She needs to earn them. Picking up my whip, I stalk around her confidently, watching her skin dot with tiny bumps. "Please, I—"

"I didn't ask you to speak. Did I?" I enquire curiously. She shakes her head slowly. Another tremble shoots through her. I raise the whip, bringing it down on her smooth thighs. A loud yelp falls from her plump lips. "No. Fucking. Noise." Her body shudders with a hiccup, and I know she's crying, even though I can't see her eyes.

With her gaze trained on the floor before her, she doesn't lift her head, but instead she sniffles quietly. I come to a stop at her knees. "Eyes up." When she obeys, lifting those chocolate orbs to meet my blue ones, my cock hardens painfully. "You're such a pretty girl when you cry."

Tears stream down her cheeks then, and I smile.

This is who I am.

When I finally accepted it—came to terms with my fate—my father looked at me with pride. For the first time in twenty long years, he regarded me as a man rather than a child. Raising the whip, I dangle it before her, showing her what lies in her future.

The pain I love inflicting and the blood I love to draw from smooth, creamy skin make me so hard—so fucking solid—that when I drive into their tight bodies, I make them scream my fucking name, over and over again.

I wasn't always like this. When I turned eighteen, it was as if suddenly the blood that coursed through my veins heated and pulsed with the need to unleash the monster within. The one hiding beneath the beds of sweet angels like this one. This is my family legacy and it has been for generations. It's part of the family business. Generations of Wolfe men came into their own doing what I'm doing right now. Making sure pretty girls earn their place.

It was two years ago when I first made a girl cry and beg. When I licked at the crimson liquid that seeped from her flesh after I whipped her, I knew—I was the man my father wanted me to be. A Wolfe. "Please, don't hurt me anymore." Her angelic voice penetrates my memories, and I glare at her. She shifts and I can tell she's uncomfortable. I realize her legs must be aching. I've had her in the kneeling position for a little while now, and she's probably not used to it. Tough. She'll have to learn somehow.

Gripping her hair, I tug her up. Her knees give out, which only serves to annoy me. "If you don't stand properly, you'll feel more pain than what I have in store for you. I'm not going to tell you again," I grunt harshly, and she shivers, which makes me hard as rock. I'm supposed to have this one for two weeks. She'll probably be my most difficult toy. I can tell from the way her body trembles to the tears that threaten to spill from those doe eyes, and I haven't even spanked her yet. Most of them cry, all of them beg and plead, but only once I've started training. My heart rate rises as I watch her lower lip wobble. "If you cry, I'll take it out on your tight little ass. Do you want that?" I hiss in her ear, and she quickly sucks in a breath.

She must still be a virgin back there, which has me imagining how deliciously tight her ass will be squeezing my dick, and that thought has me throbbing in my slacks. "Pl... please..." she mumbles again, and I can't help chuckling. They always beg, and I always deliver. Their innocence and purity will be a thing of the past. Once I'm done with them and they look in the mirror, they'll see how their light has been snuffed out.

I won't do it quickly either.

Each day of training, I slowly dim the flame—like watching someone die.

Once it's gone, they're no longer the virtuous little liars they pretend to be.

No. They're filthy little toys.

Love & Pain

At the end of innocence,
walking through the gates of hell,
I knew he was my savior.
I saw the light in his darkness.
Within love, there is pain,
but without love there is nothing.

Angel

sixteen-years-old

The tall, masked man shoves me into a large room, causing me to stumble onto my hands and knees because of the shackles on my ankles and wrists. A bitter taste from the drink I had earlier has my tongue sticking to the roof of my mouth.

Confusion clouds my mind and the images I try to recall are fuzzy. I'm not sure what happened, but as I drag my gaze around the room, I frown noticing the exquisite elegance of my surroundings. The bedroom is furnished with old antiques, and colored in rich creams, auburns, and browns. It's almost as if I've been transported to a nineteenth-century castle.

I blink, once, twice and my vision blurs.

My mind is a mess.

Images flit through my memory, but nothing makes sense.

Fear courses through me when I turn to glance up at the formidable figure. He doesn't say a word, only watches. The black mask he wears has a silver lightning streak through it over the left eye. He's older, probably my father's age, judging from the dusting of gray that peeks out from the sides of the mask, obvious even in the dim light.

"Where am I?" I question but it goes unanswered. He stalks over to the fireplace and pushes a button, which has the fake fire blazing in seconds. With a glance at me, he crooks his finger, summoning me.

I'm tempted to ignore him, but I'm not sure what his intentions for me are so I push to my feet and wobble over to him before he can say anything more. Fear overwhelms me as I near him, but I swallow it down, and steel myself for whatever is about to happen.

Suddenly, he grips the metal between my wrists and tugs me forward. A small stumble has my body flush against his, and I gasp when I feel something poking at my stomach. Leaning in, his mouth nears my ear. "You're owned now," he hisses. "You, my little princess, are going to bring us a lot of money." The menace in his tone sends fear skittering across my skin and down my spine.

A lump thickens in my throat and tears burn my eyes painfully, but I don't blink. I don't want to cry in front of him, even though I'm on the verge. He lifts me and stalks toward the bed, dropping me on the soft mattress. Without another word, he attaches the cuffs around my wrists to the headboard and my ankles to the footboard of the bed.

"Please, let me go. I just want to go home." He ignores me and continues his work.

Moments later, he turns to leave, but before he walks out the door, he glances at me and nods. And then I'm alone. I'm restrained, so I can't explore the room, but my eyes dart around. He left the fire going. The shiver that wracks my body has less to do with the temperature, and everything to do with the thoughts of what that man is going to do to me while I'm tied up and helpless.

The darkening sky outside is the only indication that it's nighttime. After long moments, my arms tingle from being in the same position for so long. Soreness and dread overwhelm me and I burst into tears.

I don't know how long I lie on the soft, plush mattress and cry, but gradually exhaustion creeps in and steals me for the night.

"Miss." A sweet voice rouses me, and the clinking of chains drags me from my slumber. "Please, miss, wake up." When I crack my eyes open, I find a young woman who looks older than me, but not by much, watching me intently. My gaze darts around to find that my legs aren't shackled anymore, but my arms are still above my head. "I was worried about you," she offers with a warm smile, but I respond with an angry glare. *What? Worried?*

"Where the hell am I?" She flinches at my words, but I don't care. Anger fuels me, and I tug my arms. They, however, don't give way and the metal bites into my sensitive skin, causing me to wince in pain.

"Please stop doing that. He'll get angry." Her big brown eyes dart toward the headboard where my hands are.

"Who are you? Why am I here? Who is he?" She shakes her head quickly and turns to the trolley behind her. There's a bucket of steamy water and a sponge with a bottle of what looks like soap.

"I need to get you ready. He'll be here soon and he doesn't like waiting. You need to be cleaned and shaven. Please, don't fight me. I'm going to help you, but you need to trust me." Her pleading gaze startles me. It's then that I take her in, allowing my gaze to roam over her. She's got smooth pale skin, but the bright blue and purple bruises on her wrists tell me she's speaking from experience.

"What's your name?" I question, hoping I'll at least get some response. A small smile plays on her lips. Her chocolate brown bangs hang low, close to wide, chestnut eyes.

"Dakota," she answers. "Just trust me, okay?"

I watch her for a while before responding. "I don't know you. I need to know what I'm doing here. Or why am I here? Please?" I plead, imploring her with my gaze. She lifts her eyes to mine. A long sigh escapes her lips and I can tell she's trying to figure out if she should tell me or not.

"I've only been told to clean you. I don't know more than that"—she quickly glances at the door and then back at me, lowering her voice—"just don't fight him. He's…"

Her words taper off, and she shakes her head.

My heart constricts in fear. "He scares me," I confess quietly, but she doesn't respond. "I need to call my parents. My father will be able to help." Once again the shake of her head answers *no*. "You're scared too," I murmur and she flits up her dark gaze.

"Please, just stop talking." This time, it's her plea that hangs between us.

Nodding, I concede wordlessly. Quietly, she proceeds to wash me. Her touch is gentle, and as she cleans me, I find solace in her caring touch. I watch in equal amounts of fear and awe as she starts shaving between my legs. I'd never even done this myself, not that I needed to, since I don't have very much down there. I also don't have a boyfriend, and most of my friends say they only do it when they know they're going to have sex.

That thought sends a new wave of fear through me. *Oh my God! Is he going to have sex with me? Is that why she's doing this?*

She straightens and clears her throat. "All done. I'll be back tonight with your dinner. Perhaps by then, he'll have untied you. He's not going to hurt you, as long as you obey him. Just remember, don't answer him back. He doesn't like it." With that my new friend turns and pushes her trolley toward the door.

"Wait!"

She halts, and when she turns to me, she shakes her head and continues out the door, leaving me alone once again. The soft scent of the soap she used hangs thick in the air around me and the fragrance reminds me of my past.

When I was little, playing in fields of lavender.

When I was happy. When I was free.

Tears burn my eyes anew, but I vow not to let him see me cry. No matter what he does to me, I'll be strong. With that thought, my mind flits to a memory of my parents.

"You're my sweet girl." I glance at my mother, taking in her wry smile. Even though her words are heartfelt, her face holds an expression of pain, and I wonder why. A soft stroke of her hand on my cheek is gentle enough to have me leaning into her touch. "Remember I'll love you always." I just turned thirteen a few days ago and she's been strange ever since.

"Of course, Mom. Why are you being so dramatic?" I roll my eyes, and she grins wistfully. Even though I wait, no answer comes, and I'm left feeling like there's something unsaid between us. Secrets, I hate them. They've been lingering in our family for so long, and I wish every day that they'd go away. Perhaps it's my innocence, but adults seem to have more problems with every secret they keep.

"Come on girls, let's go." My father steps into my bedroom, and I notice he's dressed in a suit and tie. Normally, he only dresses up when he goes to work. Although we're meant to be going out tonight, I didn't expect him to be wearing such fancy clothing. He promised he'd take me to see Swan Lake, after months of begging. I've been attending ballet since I could walk, but haven't been to class in a few days because I twisted my ankle.

"Dad, why are you dressed so fancy?" I giggle, because everyone in the room looks so serious. My mother's gaze darts to

him, and I notice something cross her features. Fear?

"Come on, pumpkin. We'll be late. I wanted to dress up for your special night." He winks in that playful way he always does, and I calm. Shaking my head of the worry, I push off the bed and race to the door. Before I get to the stairs, I hear my mother hiss, "You're really going through with this?"

My dad's response sounds angry, but he keeps his voice low. "I have no fucking choice. He asked to see her." As if his hissed words broke the tension, the air clears as he turns toward me and holds out a big, strong hand. "Tonight is special, okay, Freya?" My father loves to use my given name when he's trying to get his point across, so I nod my head, hoping that all I've noticed tonight is just my overactive imagination.

"Yes, Daddy. Stop being so serious. Let's go, we're going to be late." As we head to the car, I don't realize that tonight will set in motion events that will change my life forever.

"Wake up." A deep rumble drags me from the dream, which is more of a memory. When I open my eyes, I find the man in the mask staring down at me. His heated gaze travels over my bare body, and I shudder. Shoving up, I try to sit but my arms protest. He leans in and I shy away, but his eyes darken as he watches me. He doesn't hurt me—all he does is reach up and unlock the chains, allowing my arms to flop down to my sides.

Pins and needles tingle through my limbs, and I rub them while glaring at him. "Why am I here?" I question, hoping he'll give me an explanation, even if it's not one I want to hear. The unknown niggles at me and fear sets in as he meets my gaze.

His lips curl into a smirk, those seemingly black eyes bore into me, and even though the mask covers half his face, I can tell from the wrinkles around his mouth he's much older. "You're here to pay back a debt, princess. Now, we're going to get acquainted, little one, and you're going to bestow on me all those soft whimpers and moans I know you're hiding in that pretty little mouth." That's when I realize I have no fucking idea how I'm going to get out of here without dying first, but I vow to never stop trying. He'll have to kill me first.

Samael

twenty-seven-years-old

"Samael." The harsh voice from behind me has me pivoting to find my father stalking angrily toward me, and I know this isn't going to be good. It's been seven years since I was brought into the fold and taught that my heritage lies in the taking of souls. And since then, I've prided myself in the nickname the others have given me— the Grim Fucking Reaper.

"Is something wrong?" I question with a calm tone, relaxing my stance. I take in his body language. I can read people easily and my father is a well-known story to me. I know his every nuance. When he's angry, I can see it a mile away.

"Your sister needs to be picked up from the warehouse. The new shipment arrived and she's been overseeing it. I need you to collect her. I've got Dax doing something for me." I nod. My sister is a feisty little piece of dynamite. She may be small, but she's got one hell of a bite. Even so I don't want her near that man. He's an asshole.

"Yes, I'll go now." Without another word he turns and leaves me staring after his retreating form. It's strange that he's so wound up about this. Maybe he found out about my sister fucking his right-hand man. I saw it months ago. She's constantly down at the club when he's working. One night, I walked into my office and turned on the cameras, and there she was in all her naked glory, bound to a bed in room four. I turned it off immediately—that was a sight that would be burned into my retinas for life. My sister fucking a man older than me.

Theia is only twenty-three. She was what we called the miracle baby. My mother had me, waited two years and then Kael came along, not long after he was born, my mother and father's relationship fell apart. But two years later, they had a surprise when Mom went for a check-up and was told she was pregnant with her third baby. The one that would ultimately kill her. There were difficulties bringing my sister to term, and there were delivery complications. They said Theia had suffered with low birth weight and anemia.

She wasn't expected to live, but she shocked everyone when she fought her way out of the danger zone and recovered fully. Because of all that, they decided to name her after the Greek goddess of light. And she is. She has a light that shines in her big blue eyes, which match mine. My little sister is beautiful beyond measure, and I suppose that's why Dax is so enamored with her. Even though I think he's way too old for her, it seems they have no shame flaunting their relationship in the club and sometimes outside as well, which only pisses me off even more.

I head up to my bedroom and grab my keys. Before heading out, I check my schedule and find that I have a training session with Pixie tonight. The woman is beautiful—small and toned, with jet-black hair and big green eyes. Her arms are fully tatted and her tits are impressive on her small frame. Just the thought of her has my dick hardening.

Heading down the stairs and through the kitchen, I find our cook preparing lunch. "Hesti." I lean in and peck her on the cheek, to which she swats me away. I'm the only person who calls her that.

"Sammy, are you hungry?" she questions, turning to me with a motherly smile. This woman has been our saving grace. After Mom died, Hesta took on the role, and as much as some kids would be angry that she's trying to play Mom, we loved her more for it. I suppose we hungered for the compassion. She took charge of three children who weren't hers and she did it without complaint.

"No, I need to collect Theia from the warehouse." She nods, turning to grab something from a tray and holds out the treat to me. As I bite into the warm, delicious confection, I realize it's her famous dark chocolate chip cookies. "These are awesome. Thanks, Hesti."

Once I've practically swallowed the whole thing, I make my way out to my sleek white Maserati. It's a contrast to who I am—all black and darkness—while my sweet thing is white and pure. If I can find a woman as virginal as my car, I'd fuck her into submission and marry her.

As quickly as the thought crosses my mind, I stifle it.

Marriage isn't in the cards for me. I'm in this life and there's no getting out. My father made it clear, the only way to get out is if you die. Wolfe Enterprises has its finger in many honeypots—I chuckle at the analogy—and there's no way you can walk away after you learn what goes on. Even though we have an upstanding business, importing and exporting electronic goods, it's what goes on beneath the cover of darkness that's the real moneymaker.

My father owns Caged—one of the most talked about underground BDSM clubs in the country—and the only clients we have are the vilest of men with the sickest fantasies and cravings.

Famous, wealthy, and filthy—from politicians, to police officers, even assholes who put their pretty faces on big screens across the world. They're all regular patrons of Caged. They walk in to have their forbidden fantasies played out. *And me?* I'm the dark fucking prince who has been called on to train the girls to obey, pleasure, and submit. Each girl goes through a process and I, along with three other men, make sure they're ready for what lies in those rooms.

Each client maintains his anonymity by wearing a mask. All the trainers, including myself, wear our own branded mask when we're working. None of the girls will ever see our faces.

I've been the most successful at breaking each toy I've

been gifted to train.

Each one of them is perfectly submissive and can take any form of punishment.

That's why they call me the Grim Reaper.

I take beautiful, sweet, innocent girls and taint their innocent souls. I kill everything they hold dear—that pure virtue every girl possesses.

A toy to use as the clients wish.

As I weave my way through the traffic, I wonder what would happen if someone did that to Theia. I'd probably hunt the fuckers down and kill them. Slice them limb from limb. Isn't that ironic, I've become the type of person I would love to kill. And I wouldn't think twice about doing it.

Pulling up to the warehouse, I find it busier than I thought. The crew is filling two gigantic trucks with boxes which I can only guess include televisions, DVD players, and the toys my father imports for resale. They are all made in South America. When they reach us, we distribute to a number of stores across the country.

"Sammy!" My sister bounds up to me and jumps into my arms. "Where is Dax?" she questions with a pout, and I shake my head in response.

"Do not let Dad hear you asking about him. And he's busy, anyway." She releases me from her hold and steps back, regarding me with frustration. I've warned her off him too many times to count, but my sister is as stubborn as I am.

"You're just grouchy that you're still single. You need a girl in your life." Her retort comes with a playful swat which earns her a narrowed stare.

"I'm not grouchy. All I want is for you to be safe. I don't need you dating someone who's old enough to be your father. It's just weird."

"He's not that old," she gasps. "What if you met a girl who's young and beautiful? Would you say the same thing?" I head into the warehouse before answering her.

"It's not the same thing." Her heels click behind me, and I can feel her burning a hole in my back with her pretty blue eyes, which seem to glow with a gemstone light at times. "You're my sister, and I need to protect you from assholes."

"Dax is not an asshole. He's sweet and kind and he treats me like a princess." I turn to regard her and see the emotion in her expression. She's falling for him.

"So you've submitted to a man who Father will kill if he were to find out." My heart rate kicks up at the thought of my sister becoming like the girls I train. Turning into the type of girl that I yearn for—a submissive who will kneel for me when I bid her.

"Sam, I'm not a child anymore. If he wants to disown me the way he did with Kael, then so be it. I'll be better off without him in my life. It's my choice and I will do what I want. Now, let's go home. I'm hungry and I have work to do." She responds without actually answering the question I asked. She spins on her heel and leaves me gaping at her back. *Fuck! Why do women have to be so frustrating?*

Your Light

The light that shines through your cracks never dims.
It's then that I see love.
It's then that I find happiness.
Even in our darkness, you blind me with your light.

Angel

two years later

"You're an incredibly beautiful girl, pet," he slurs in my ear, sending revulsion through me. "Tonight, I want to see how well your tight little ass handles a ten-inch dildo. Then you're going to swallow my cock." A chuckle, which has my body quivering with fear and my spine tingling with panic, falls from his cracked lips. "Too bad I can't rip your cherry from you. I'd love to see you bleed on my cock."

The rope around my wrists tightens as he tugs me to my feet. He remains silent as he leads me to the bed, which is covered in the finest crimson silk sheets. I climb onto the mattress without his order, because I know what he wants. This isn't the first time he's done this, and somehow I know it won't be the last.

"Kneel, head down, ass up," he growls with such perverse lust I feel it in my bones. "I want these precious arms between *your legs." Once again, he pulls on the thick binding, which bites into my sensitive skin, and proceeds tying my wrists to my ankles, leaving me at his mercy. But as always, there'll be none.*

The cold steel of a blade taunts my skin as it slithers its way down my thighs, like a venomous snake readying itself to strike. Dread grips my chest and breathing becomes difficult. "Such a pretty little slut with beautiful holes I'm going to use." The tip of the knife he wields trails under the delicate material of the panties that cover my most intimate area. When it falls away, the cold air hits my core and I stifle the gasp by biting my lip so hard, a metallic taste fills my mouth.

It's silent for a while, and then I hear it — the swish of leather echoing loudly in my ears. Then it starts.

One. Two. Three.

Blinding pain lashes my back and ass. The whip licks against the smooth lips of my pussy, stinging as it continues its attack on my flesh.

Four. Five. Six.

"Fucking little whore! Cry for me." He goads me into it every time. It's as if he needs my tears to feel like a man. His face is hidden behind a mask, but I don't need to see it to know that he is the devil. Satan himself. Evil hangs heavy in the air that swirls around him, following him around like a cloud. An aura.

Seven. Eight. Nine.

He stops for a beat and waits for it, but I don't give in. I don't allow myself to offer him my tears. He may hurt me, he may make me bleed, but he'll never possess me.

Ten. Eleven. Twelve.

The whip drops onto the plush carpet. His footfalls fade, and the sound of matches send anxiety over every inch of my skin. "You can fight it all you want, little one, you'll cry. I will make sure of it," he vows with salacious intent. "The men you'll be meeting soon want those pretty tears. That's why you're here. To give them what they can't have at home. Those pretty little princesses, all dressed up in shiny dresses with innocence dripping from them, can't be touched, but you,"—he strokes a finger over my core—"you're going to fulfill men's desires."

Without warning, he slams a smooth, long object into my dry pussy, and I cry out so loud I wish there were neighbors nearby to hear me. He continues his assault, plunging in and out. I can't tell what it is, but the edge bites into my inner walls, sending searing pain shooting through me.

"Oh, how I'd love to really break you in, princess." His words are filled with wonderment, and I'm confused about their meaning. "To make this tight little cunt all woman. To see your beautiful crimson blood marking this candle. But I won't, because if I do, I won't get paid." The sound of a match being struck booms around me as if it's on a surround-sound speaker system. "Let it all burn away, sweetheart. You may be a virgin, but you're no longer innocent."

At that very moment, as his words seep into my mind, I fear I may never get back what I've lost. I've been in this hell for a year and as much as I've tried to be strong, each time he's hurt me, every time he brings me in here, it's carved into my heart. The pain and fear have broken me. The only thing I hold onto is my soul. And deep down I grieve. I cry inwardly. Shutting my eyes tight, I let all my emotions tumble and twirl in my chest. The tears he promised flow freely down my cheeks, but he'll not hear me cry.

Hot liquid drips onto my puckered entrance and the scent

of flowers hits my senses, causing me to retch at the sweet fragrance in this utterly vile room. The buzzing of the dildo he promised taunts me before I'm filled painfully, and it feels as if I'm being ripped in two. The agony is beyond anything I've ever felt. "Gorgeous. Just fucking perfect. Do you feel that, princess? One day soon, this will be a man inside you. Don't you like that? You'll be a whore, only good for one thing. A toy for men to use for pleasure." With that, he continues plunging the plastic cock into my ass, faster and deeper until I feel a sticky splatter on my back, and I know he's just come all over my ass.

Music drifts from the closed door dragging me from the memory of what he did to me on my seventeenth birthday. Here I stand, eighteen years old, an adult, and a man I've never seen is still holding me prisoner.

As the melodies filter through the grate in the wall, I hear the laughter of the *guests*. He's coming for me. He always does. Pulling on the robe, I tie my hair into a bun, and I apply the gloss to my lips, like he told me. It's been two long years since he brought me to this room. Since the night I was stolen from my family. It's been two long years, and even though he's not taken my virginity, he's hurt me in many other ways. I know tonight will not be any different.

The door opens and he walks in. His smirk sends an eerie feeling skittering across my skin, and I can't stop the tremble. As much as I try to stay strong, he has a way of getting to me. Slithering beneath the surface, poisoning me with just a wicked glare.

"There's my little princess." He's taken to calling me

that, and I hate it. Never has he used my real name, and I wonder if he knows who I am. Of course he does, he bought me, or *stole* me. I don't know what happened. To this day, he hasn't given me so much as an inkling of why or how I ended up here. All he's told me is that I'm here to pay off a debt. Whose? I may never know. "Tonight is special. You're eighteen, and after two years of waiting, you're ready to begin your training and get to work." He smiles as he tells me this. In all the times he's been in here and hurt me, he's never given me a genuine smile. Yet it's even more sinister than his evil grins.

"What do you mean?" It's stupid to question, but I do anyway.

My captor—the stranger—stares at me with amusement dancing in those dark eyes. He's in a good mood. At least there's no tension radiating off him. The mask he's worn every time I've seen him is in place. Taunting me by hiding his identity. "Tonight you'll meet your new Master or shall I say, owner. He's pleased with the videos he's seen of you. You'll be going home with him this evening."

His words send fear coursing through me and panic flaring in my chest. "No, I mean, why—"

With two long strides he closes the distance between us and instantly his hand is around my throat. "If you so much as utter one negative thing, I'll be forced to snuff you out. Don't fucking tempt me. Because before I do, I'll make sure that cute little body of yours is ruined so badly, they won't even recognize your corpse," he hisses in my face with venom dripping off each word.

Tears prick my eyes, and I have to blink them back. If he sees me crying now, I'll be in a lot more pain than I was before. Silently, he fastens the thin silver collar around my neck, which sparkles with jewels that probably cost more than my life. The leash attached to it gets yanked, and I stumble behind him, slamming into his solid back.

Stay calm. Please. Don't hurt me.

My mind is on a constant loop, begging and pleading, hoping that the pain won't come. But deep down I know that wherever I'm headed will be far worse than anything he's put me through.

"Come on, princess." He tugs again, and I follow unwillingly behind his confident strides. The long hallway, which is lit by ornate chandeliers and is adorned with artwork hanging on both sides, leads to a foyer. But there's no exit. It's as if I'm in the wing of a mansion. The spiral staircase before us leads toward a double-glass door. The house itself has so many windows, I wonder if he's not afraid of people seeing what he does. The grounds of the house stretch for miles surrounded by a forest that looks inviting, not that I've ever been allowed outside.

The doors glide open as we step into what would normally be a cellar, at least that's what I would call it, but the area's been refurbished. Instead of a dank and dreary room, it resembles a five-star restaurant. "I see the star of the show has arrived." A man—one also hidden by a mask, one that resembles a wolf with a similar silver streak through one eye, like that of my captor's—stalks up to me and reaches for my face. I can't stop my instinctive flinch in response.

My gaze flits between the two men, and I wonder if they're brothers. They're both older from what I can tell, with the fine wrinkles around their mouths and thick heads of salt and pepper hair that can't be hidden by the masks. "You scared of me, pet?" He chuckles with a filthy leer that travels from my collar to my chest, as if he's trying to see through material of the shift dress I'm wearing. I've lived in fear since I arrived here. Not having a moment where I was comfortable, no matter how beautiful the room I was locked in was. But something about the man before me has terror burrowing into my core.

"She's pure, beautiful, and trust me when I say, delicious." The man who's owned me for the last two years boasts to his friend. If only I could see their faces. But instead, I'm left clueless as to who these evil men are.

"I'll have to have a taste. Won't I, pet?" His hand reaches between my legs and thick fingers probe at my sex. My body shudders in fear, and the hunger in his dark eyes is evident. "Smooth cunt, I like that." I know he's not talking to me, but his gaze is on me when he rips the panties I'm wearing away from my hips. His fingers plunge inside me, pumping in and out slowly, even though his touch does nothing and the burning sensation brings tears to my eyes.

He drags his digits from my core and brings them to his lips. I turn away, but my owner forces my head back, preventing me from looking away. Watching a man old enough to be my father lick my juices from his fingers has bile burning my throat.

His eyes dart behind me, and he smiles. It's what I

would picture Satan to look like—dark, filthy, and vile. "You're right. Pure and delicious. I can't wait to make you bleed on my cock. Would you like that, princess? To feel a man inside this tight little cunt?" He forces his fingers inside me again and pumps a few times. "Soon, I'll take that thing you hold dear. Your virginity will be mine. I'll fucking own it. And every time a man drives his hard cock inside you, it will be me you feel." His vow is filled with salacious intent, which only serves to disgust me further. I can't stop the retch in my throat.

Fear skyrockets my heart rate and the tears I had been holding back all this time finally escape and stream silently down my cheeks. "No. Please..." The plea falls from me as it always does, but I know it's no use. You'd think that after two years of being here I would have learned, but I haven't.

I'm still a little girl.

I miss my family.

I need my daddy to save me.

But he won't. Because deep down, I've come to the conclusion that they've killed him.

My body being jostled wakes me, and I roll over to find myself in the back seat of a car. When I try to move, my body aches and I realize my hands are bound behind me and my ankles are tied against the door handle, inhibiting my movement.

My mind is fuzzy. All I remember is the party. There

was a man—no, there were many men. I don't feel an ache between my legs, but the pain shooting through my limbs and ribs tell me they did other things. So many horrid acts that I don't want to think about. My throat is dry. My eyes well with tears and they burn, threatening to spill. I've promised myself that I'll be strong. But isn't there a point when life hands us too much? When you've just endured everything you can and it finally fills your cup, overflowing into unwanted tears you've hidden away. That's how I feel.

"Where…?" The word is a croak at best, and the man in the driver's seat glances at me in the rear view mirror. I can't see his face. It's distorted by a mask.

They all hide. All the evil lies behind a piece of plastic. Why can't they grow a pair and show themselves? "I'm Hazard, at least, that's what they call me. I'm taking you home, little one. There's a special room waiting for you," he tells me on a smirk. Those pretty words of going home don't mean what I pray they do, instead they hold vile promises. His voice is different—not that of the same man who held me in the room. This one seems different somehow, younger perhaps.

It's dark, so I can't make out anything about the car, except that there are red lights on the dashboard. "Why do they want me?" I question again, hoping to make sense of what's happening to me.

It's been too long. I've been stolen, kidnapped, and nobody has even looked for me. My father is, or was, a powerful man, surely he'd have found me by now. Unless they've really hurt him. Unless my fear that he's dead is true.

"Because you're going to make the boss man a lot of money," he confides. I recognize it instantly. In a world of pain and punishment, the emotion has me reeling. Guilt. Why would he feel guilty? I don't understand. "Your trainer is waiting on you. He's the best. He'll take you and make sure your pretty little body is ready. You see, sweetheart, some people in this life are out for payment, perhaps not monetary, but physical. The boss man is in charge, and what he wants, he gets, unfortunately. Your innocence is like a drug to them. They crave it, just like your trainer will. We call him the Grim Reaper, but don't tell him I told you. That will spoil all the fun." He chuckles at his last few words, but the name has stuck in my mind. *The Grim Reaper.* More fear engulfs me, and I wonder why Hazard told me things I don't think he should be telling me. "I think he's going to be quite enamored with you." His words are laced with amusement.

"Fuck you," I spit at him. My throat burns with the food I was forced to eat last night and my stomach churns with hate. His laugh may sound carefree, but it's only an act. He's probably as bad as the man he stole me from. Maybe worse. I'll find a way out. And if they have more girls, I'll save them too.

"Oh, the time for all that will come. I promise you. I only wish I was the one ripping apart those precious holes of yours, but alas, you're not mine sweetheart. You're his, and he likes when girls scream. I bet you'll sound like a siren when you cry and beg for him to stop. Won't you?"

Eyes dart to me in the reflection of the mirror, and I can see a flicker of something in the dim light, perhaps hunger, desire, but I can't make out what exactly.

I don't offer him a response. He doesn't deserve it. What he does deserve is to die. And I swear on my life I'll make sure that happens.

Anger burns like a flame inside me. Fury heats my blood, and I make a vow to myself while on this seat as my body gets thrown around by the road we're traveling on—I'll make sure all of them pay. In ugly, torturous ways.

The car suddenly hits smoother road and then we're cruising down winding curves. I know this because my body sways back and forth.

A distant creak of a gate sounds, and I realize we've reached hell. He drives us through, and in the darkness I pray for light. For something, or someone to save me. The car stops and my captor gets out, leaving me lying in silence. My ears prick, and I hear him talk to someone just outside.

"Dax, boss wants you to put our newest acquisition in her bedroom. She'll be introduced to her trainer in the morning. The short drive from the east wing was easy enough. She was passed out cold," he informs the new stranger, and I wonder what he means by "east wing." *Am I still on the same property?* If so, there must be a way out. I'll find it somehow.

"Sure thing, Hazard," another man answers. A second later, my body is ripped from the car as the door which has my feet bound to it opens and big strong hands tug me. "Come on, little one, time to get some sleep. Tomorrow you meet your trainer."

I'm thrown over a shoulder and I wiggle in an attempt to get free, but it's no use.

"You're a spitfire. I'm sure he'll have loads of fun with you." The man, who I assume is Dax, guffaws as he walks through a doorway and heads down a long, dark hallway. All too soon, I hear a click and suddenly I'm dumped onto a bed. When I finally get a good look at Dax, I can't stop the gasp that falls from my lips.

He's probably six feet or more of pure muscle. With his long, light brown hair, that's buzzed short on the sides, and a thick beard covering his prominent jaw, he looks scary. And that doesn't even include the sleeves of tattoos that adorn his thick arms, which meet dangerous looking knuckles.

"Why me? What are they going to do to me?" The questions fall from my lips again while he proceeds to untie me.

"Don't ask too many questions and you may get out alive," he explains in a lowered tone. "You need to trust your maker." His cryptic words don't stop the flurry of anxiety that sends my stomach into disarray. "Now, get some sleep. Tomorrow is a big day for you."

Even though he is one of the scariest men I've ever seen, there is a disarming honesty that shines from his eyes. Deep pools of ice blue settle on me, but it's not the color that gives him away, it's the emotion that flits through them when he regards me.

"Who is my maker?" I ask in confusion. He doesn't respond, but merely grins, and with that, I'm left alone in the room with my mind whirling at a thousand miles a minute.

Samael

"Brother, I had a taste of your new pet last night," I tell him as he gets ready. Leaning on the doorjamb of his bedroom, I watch his reaction.

"And? Is she sweet?" he growls out, and I know I've gotten to him. He's so compassionate and gentle for a Dom, or a Master, I don't know how he does this.

"Fucking delectable. She made me so hard, I almost took her right there in her garden. I bet she's still a virgin from the way she moaned when I sucked on her tongue." He shudders, but tries to hide it.

"Great, I'm glad you had your fun. Now it's my turn." He pulls on the hoodie he normally hides behind and stalks past me, but before he disappears down the hallway, I get in my last threat.

"Make her bleed, brother, because if you don't, I will."

He's probably going to taste her sweet cunt. I was so fucking *tempted to take her last night, to fuck her hard and rough. She'd allow me to. I felt her body respond to me. They all do. But she's not mine. She's Kael's toy. The beautiful redhead. A firebird if ever I saw one.*

I know if I took her, it would anger him and I do love to do that.

I've always taunted him. Even now that we're grown up, I still do it.

"Sam," a gruff voice calls me, dragging me from the memory of taunting my brother only two years ago. I turn to regard my father. He's a formidable man who people bow down to. All he has to do is cast them one of his stern glares.

"Father."

"I've got someone I'd like you to meet. Best to mask yourself. She's new, and I'd like her to fear you rather than get attached. You know how the new girls tend to find you alluring," he remarks with frustration. It's true, I've had two girls grow rather attached to me. I tend to walk in the same circles as most of their families, those who are still alive, and if they recognize me, it will be the end of this charade. In this game, anonymity is our biggest weapon. If they don't know us, they can't find out about what we do.

I've been doing this for too long.

Shaking my head of that thought, I pull on my mask and follow my father from my office down the hall to his.

I can't wait to sink my teeth into her. Everyone calls me the Grim Reaper because I break girls in record time. I take those untainted souls and darken them, bit-by-bit, bringing out the filthy little sluts hiding below their virtuous veneer.

Murdering the sweet, angelic princesses.

As we enter the parlor, I see the tiny blonde on her knees. She's dressed in a pretty white dress with a pattern of small flowers. Her hair hangs down to her shoulder blades, wavy and shimmery, almost gold in hue. I notice her hands fiddling with something on her lap. "Who's this?" I ask my father as my curiosity piques.

"She doesn't have a name anymore. She's eighteen, although she looks like she's sixteen, which the clients will love." His voice is filled with humor, but I'm not listening. I'm intrigued by the little beauty at my feet. She's pure. Reeking of virginity, like an angel.

"Eyes up, Angel," I command, and she obeys without hesitation. *Fucking perfect.* Her eyes are similar to Paige's. The color of tourmaline—a deep green gemstone— shimmering as if they're taunting me. Every thought of the fire-haired beauty from my memories from earlier leaves me when I take in the woman kneeling before me. Her smooth skin is creamy and free of make up. She regards me with wariness, but there's a fire dancing in her gaze. It's beautiful. Intoxicating to see a girl in a place like this with so much fight still blazing through her. Although her posture is submissive, I can read the courage she hides. I'm not sure why she's hiding, but I'll find out soon enough.

No pet has enamored me like this. Perhaps it's her natural beauty. Most of the toys Father brings in here are too made up, like porcelain dolls. This one… She's different.

When I reach for her face, she flinches, it's a slight movement but I pick up on it. Brushing my knuckles along her cheek, I tip my head to the side as electricity shoots through me. A connection—one I've never felt with any woman before—jolts me. There's a pull between us, and when I meet her eyes dead on, I know she feels it too.

I crouch before her and grab the collar that adorns her slim neck. I tug it forward until her face is inches from mine. Our eyes are locked in a heated exchange, and I see the flames raging behind hers. I'm going to dowse it, one fucking spark at a time. And when I'm done, she'll be mine.

Broken and tainted.

Used and abused.

She'll ache to be taken rough and hard.

I'll pull the little masochist out of her and when I'm done, I'll claim her. Her lips pout in the cutest display of stubbornness, and I'm tempted to own her. Everything in my chest craves it. But I'll have to wait. She can't be mine yet.

"Come." I pull the ring of her collar and she obeys, crawling behind me. "I'll see you later, Father. I'm going to see how well this one takes instruction." He nods, stepping aside allowing me to disappear down the hallway with my new toy.

When we reach my room, I push the door open and step inside.

Various gray hues greet us, but the most prominent is black.

Shades of darkness that speak to my soul.

I don't like color.

That's a lie.

I love red. Blood red.

I love the color of crimson when it's seeping from creamy skin.

I watch Angel crawl into the room, and when I shut the door with a click, I see her tremble.

Beautiful.

"Stand and strip." With intoxicating grace, she rises and slowly pushes the sleeves of her dress over her shoulders. As it pools at her feet, I take in the innocent underwear that covers her breasts and pussy. White. "Are you a virgin?" I question with curiosity lacing my tone, and when her eyes meet mine, I notice the trepidation swirling in them.

"Yes, Sir," she murmurs, but her eyes flit nervously between mine and the window, which convinces me there's something she's not telling me. Even so, the words have my dick throbbing. Aching to drive into her tight, untouched pussy. To feel her body pulse and stretch around me as I break that sweet innocence.

Her submissiveness is clearly ingrained in her demeanour. Whoever it was that trained her must have resorted to other punishments. Perhaps violence? Tipping my head to the side, I regard her fidgeting. "Tell me, Angel. Have you had a man in your mouth, or that pert ass?"

She lifts her chin then, and a little bit of that fire I saw earlier comes blazing back. "Yes, I have. Why?" The confidence in her answer angers me. Not because of her feistiness, but because she's already been violated. Why would I care? I shouldn't.

Shaking my head of the errant thoughts, I respond, "You're well trained. There's only one explanation that would make sense. A man must have hurt you to make sure you're obedient. Tell me what happened?"

Fear flits across her features, but she steels herself and stares at me before answering. "I was kidnapped when I turned sixteen. He taught me to be obedient in ways I'd rather not talk about. He never fucked me in the two years I was there. At first I thought it was because I wasn't of age, but then one day he confessed it was because he wouldn't get paid if he'd taken my virginity."

The word *fucked* coming from her is like an aphrodisiac. However, this is news to me. I don't know any man in this business who would just allow a virgin to stay innocent even if he was getting paid. I've known some evil, sadistic bastards. Cocking my head to the side, I regard her before asking, "I want you to tell me what he did to you." It's an order, one she can't refuse. If she's as well-trained as I know she is, she'll have to tell me. I grip the ring of her collar and make my way toward the wingback chair near my terrace. I settle myself in the plush material and pull her to kneel before me. "I'm sure he showed you how to pleasure a man?" She nods. "I want you to stroke me while you tell me. Everything."

"But—"

"Angel, don't make me ask you twice. I don't like repeating myself. Do you understand?" Another quick nod and she unzips my slacks. With tentative fingers she pulls them down along with the tight boxer briefs. Her eyes widen at the thick, angry erection jutting in her direction. *That's right, sweetheart, it's all yours.*

Her hand is warm as she wraps it around my shaft and strokes me up and down. When her thumb teases the tip, I bite down on my lip to stifle a groan.

As if her touch is a drug, my vision is locked on this beauty and only her. Thoughts of my other pets, or any woman for that matter, vanish. Angel is the only one I see. The only one I crave.

Quickly gripping her wrist, I meet her questioning gaze. "Tell me."

A shudder rolls over her body and she nods.

"The day I was taken was my sixteenth birthday. I asked my mom to drop me off at the mall so I could go shopping. I wasn't there for very long when I was pulled into what I thought was a storage closet. Only, it was a room which led out to the back of the mall." She teases the crown of my dick as she tells me the story. Her hands move almost expertly for such a young girl. She's my youngest yet. Eighteen. "He pushed me against the brick wall and told me not to make a noise. His hands groped my breasts and he pressed his…" Her words taper off, and I see the glistening on her lashes. She takes a deep breath and continues, "His dick against me. He told me I was a slut for making him hard."

I listen intently. Even though I feel like severing his head from his shoulders, she's turning me on. Just the way she carries herself. Her voice, those beautiful green eyes. And her golden waves that frame an angelic face.

"He tied me up in a bedroom of opulence and trained

me with—"

"Stop. Massage my balls, Angel." She watches me while her other hand holds the heavy sac in her tiny grasp. "Look at me," I command. Dragging her gaze to mine, she smiles when I tip her head with my index finger. "You're pretty. I'd like to own you." She opens her mouth, then shuts it again.

"I don't think…" Her words taper off, and I grasp her hand that's tight around my cock. Stroking myself with her hand, I smile kindly. However, all the thoughts running through my head are far from kind. I want to fuck her and make her bleed. I want to see that sweet innocence on my dick and I want to do it right now.

"No, you shouldn't think. You should nod, smile, and let me take you. Because I'm one of the nice men in here. Granted, I will hurt you, I'll make you bleed, but I'll also make you soar. Do you want to fly, Angel?"

I can't believe the shit I'm spewing. I'm not the nice guy. My brother is. Kael is the sweet, loving Dom. I'm the sick, sadistic bastard. And as much as I want this girl to be mine, I know I'm only training her for someone else. Better she learns the amount of pain comes with working for my father.

An image of Paige's blood dripping from her lip when I bit it flashes through my mind, and my body flames with hunger. "Stand." The pretty blonde obeys and rises. I grip her hips and spin her so her back is facing me. Pressing a hand at the base of her spine, I force her down so she's bent at the waist. Fuck, I'd love her in a spreader bar right now, but I'm too turned on.

The sunset streams through the window, shimmering on her golden hair, making her look even more angelic, but filthy as her ass taunts me. "Open your legs," I grunt, and as she does, I grip her pure white panties and rip them from her slim hips.

She doesn't stifle her gasp, which makes me smile. I palm her pert ass cheeks and spread them taking in the smoothness of her cunt and her puckered entrance. "You're bare." It's more of a statement, but comes out as a question.

"Yes, he wanted me like that." I know why the sick bastard wanted her to look like a little girl. This only serves to inflame my anger, and I'm about to break her virginity in an angry, hateful fuck. Best to be brutal from the get go.

"You're going to have to hold on to something, Angel, because this isn't going to be gentle." Another soft gasp falls from her lips as I guide her closer to the window. There are raven-colored metal vines welded to the panes, which she grips. "Good girl." I rain down harsh slaps on her ass cheeks, again and again, each fleshy globe turning blood red.

My cock is so hard, throbbing with an ache to drive deep.

To mold her body for me.

She'll only want me, need me, crave me.

Mine.

The idea pops into my head suddenly, and I swallow it down like a bitter pill.

I've never owned one girl before. Never allowed myself to have anything more than the toys I train, but there's something about this one that's bringing out something primal in me.

What I'm about to do is forbidden.

I was only supposed to let her suck me off, but this can be our secret. I tease my fingers over her lips and stroke her slowly. Teasing the arousal from her virgin cunt. *Fuck, that's so good.* I plunge one finger in to find my expert touch is no match for her, she's soaked. With my wet digits, I rub the juices from her over the tip of my cock before plunging into her in one brutal thrust.

The scream that comes from her is agonizing and it makes me harder than I've been in a long time. I don't relent, pulling out and driving back in. Her heat is beautifully erotic. Her grip on the metal turns her knuckles white. The sounds that fall from her lips are like fuel to me. I slow down then, attempting to savor her, even though it's taking all my restraint. Her body is exceptionally tight and I know I've broken her. I've taken what I wasn't meant to.

But something about this girl has gripped me. I pull out, sliding back in gently. Reaching around, I circle her clit with my thumb. For some reason, I want this to be good, even though I know it's painful for her. My hips move rhythmically. In the reflection of the window, I can see her tear-stained cheeks. Her eyes glisten, but she holds on. She takes it.

Her strength is incredible. None of the other girls I've had before have been this exquisite. This addictive. Because as I slide out and back in, taunting her clit and teasing her rosy nipples, I can feel her body pulsing in response.

Moments pass and I continue my assault on her. She's still wet. And with each drive into her, I feel the arousal from her tight cunt drench me as I plunge into her. I want her to remember this. To remember me.

Her whimpers of pain turn to moans of pleasure and I realize my little pet is loving my dick. I should have sheathed myself. But there's nothing more I want than to feel her slick walls tightening around me.

I need this.

I need her.

"Do you like that, baby?" She nods, and I grip her long blonde hair, tugging her back. "I asked you a fucking question." I hiss in her ear as I plow her tight body.

"Yes, Sir," she whimpers as my hips slap against her ass. The sound of a harsh, rough fuck echoes through my cavernous room. My balls tighten, and I reach around, tugging her throbbing little clit.

"Come for me," I order, and she does. She fucking detonates around me, and I feel her arousal soaking my cock, balls, and thighs. "You're a dirty little slut, aren't you? Coming on my cock like a common whore," I growl as my release locks my body, and I fill her with my hot seed.

The Hunter & The Angel

The hunter and the angel,
An unlikely pairing.
Within my chaos and anguish,
You were my truth, my salvation,
my heaven in hell

Angel

one year later

"When you come, you'll only do so on command. Do you understand?" His gaze penetrates me in such a way that I feel naked. As if my soul is laid out on the table for him. Allowing him to pick and prod at it and judge the torment I've been through, but he doesn't. All he shows me is his own form of kindness. Something I'm not accustomed to.

Yes, he does hurt me. There's no doubt that I ache and bleed and I have bruises, but it's when his touch is gentle that it hurts the most. Because what he doesn't realize is that he's carving me out, piece by fragmented piece. With his left hand, he reaches for my core, deft fingers stroke my slick sex and he starts the torture.

This is the worst. Holding my orgasm until he's satisfied, until he orders me to come. Everything south of my belly button tightens in the familiar way he always brings to my body.

"I'm going to take you, Angel, and ruin every inch of this perfect little body." His fingers pump in and out, his thumb circles my clit, teasing it relentlessly as he makes his promise. "I'll make certain you crave only me. And when those fuckers touch you, when they have their filthy hands on you"—his teeth graze my earlobe before he detonates me—"it will be me you think about to get you through it. Do you understand me?" I try nodding, but his hand is wrapped so tightly around my neck I can hardly move an inch.

Fire blazes in his eyes and the side of his mouth lifts into a sinful smirk. "Good girl, now come for me," he orders, tugging on the nipple clamps that bite into my hardened sensitive buds. I cry out, screaming over and over in the haze of my orgasm. I feel something dripping from me, and when I look down, my cheeks heat with embarrassment.

"I'm... I'm..." His index finger reaches under my chin, lifting my head so we're eye level with each other.

"You're fucking perfect, my little squirter." He praises me like I've just won him the jackpot. My brows furrow in confusion. I'm such a novice that I have no idea what he means, but before I can voice my concern, he lifts his hand—drenched in my fluids—and licks every drop.

"You're delicious," he declares on a sinful smirk. The way he's looking at me has me aching for more of that filthiness he delves out. When he steps back to regard me, the smirk on his perfect mouth falls and is replaced with something akin to hunger.

"Sir." The word falls easily from my lips, and it has his beautiful cobalt orbs boring into me. "I need more." Once again, the look he gives me is one of shock, but also desire. I know he *wants me as much as I want him.*

"Soon, my little Angel, I promise you. When I take you, it will be when I say, not when you do. Remember, as much as I enjoy you begging, I'm the one in control."

I nod, but regard him with a smile. "I trust you." It's been a long year and we've been back and forth more times than I care to count, but those words I've just given him mean more than anything I've ever said in my life. Because I do trust him. I'm giving him the one thing every man in here wants. The one thing clients pay for but never receive.

He's getting it on a silver platter.

I'm giving it freely.

The one thing I know he'd kill for.

Me.

With a quick glance to the corner of my room, I notice the red light blinking, which means he's watching me. It's been a year since he took me in his bedroom and told me he wanted to own me. Even though I was young, I knew exactly what he meant and it should've repulsed me, but it didn't. He didn't.

The stockings I pull up to my thighs are sheer black, and I clip them to the garter belt that hugs my hips. Every time he walks into my room, I feel the desire dripping from every pore on his beautiful body. He hasn't taken me again and I wonder if it's because he's not allowed to, or if he's biding his time.

Every night when I'm alone, I imagine him touching me again. The "work" they've assigned me is simple. All I have to do is dance upstairs in the club. The other girls have taught me some moves, but there's something about just losing myself in the music that sets me at ease.

He's always there, though.

Watching.

As if he does really own me.

"Are you ready?" I jump at the deep tone behind me. Spinning in the red heels that adorn my feet, I find him leaning against the doorjamb. His arms are folded in front of his broad chest as he regards me with that familiar hungry glare.

He has the most piercing blue eyes I've ever seen. They disarm and unnerve me, flitting between annoyance and hunger. With a slow step into my room, he shuts the door and when the lock clicks, my breathing hitches.

He's never been alone with me in my room with the door closed. Without warning, he reaches up and pulls the mask from his head. It's the first time I've come face to face with my captor.

The wolf.

To say that he's handsome would do him an injustice.

He is beautiful.

Breathtaking even.

His hair is short, cropped close to his head. His jaw is chiseled and angular and his nose is straight, giving him a regal profile. And those lips. My God those lips. His lower one is full and taunts me, making me want to bite it. His upper lip is the perfect Cupid's bow. Always curled into either a sinful smirk or a dark scowl, he regards me with a look that sets my body on fire.

He isn't clean-shaven. There's a slight hint of stubble,

and from that and the short hair on his head, I knew he had dark brown, coffee-colored hair. Smooth, lightly tanned skin greets me and beautifully alluring eyes regard me. The man is perfect. Sculpted, I'm certain, from porcelain. An innate need to kneel for him tugs at me.

He looks like he could be the next James Bond, dressed in his expensive suit.

"Are you finished gawking?" His lips quirk with amusement, and I realize I've been blatantly staring at him for too long.

"You'd be so lucky," I squeak, as I turn to face the mirror, fiddling with my hair. As I tug it to the side, I feel his warmth behind me. He reaches for the long blonde waves and settles them over my right shoulder, allowing his chin to rest lightly on my left.

The stubble on his jaw tickles my sensitive skin as he responds, "I am so lucky, Angel. Did you forget that I know what you feel like around my dick?" The question forces a gasp to fall from my lips as he presses his erection against my ass. It takes all my restraint not to push back against him. He's the only man I've been with who I want more of.

"How could I? You ruined me that day." My words still him and his body tenses behind me. "Because now I want only your *dick* inside me." As the last word falls from my lips, he grips my hips painfully and pulls my body against his. The ache between my thighs flares to life, angry and unbidden, and all I want is for him to ease it.

"You want me, Angel? Do you think you can handle me?" he growls against my neck, sending a wave of flutters through me and goose bumps dot my skin. Our gazes lock in the mirror, and I watch his eyes darken. "Watch me," he commands, and I obey.

Watching his hand trail its way down my flat belly, I whimper when he cups my pussy with his big, strong hand. "I—"

"I said watch, don't speak." My mouth shuts quickly as I observe the expert fingers of my captor tease my sex over the black panties that adorn my hips. "Good girl."

Two words.

They dispel every fear in my mind, and I moan when his middle finger finds my drenched entrance.

"Angel, when I take you again, you'll never be the same. You'll hate me when I fuck you. You'll curse me when I make you come. And you'll want to rip my heart out when I make you scream my fucking name. You know why?"

Words evade me, so I shake my head quickly.

"Because I'll fucking ruin your body. I'll destroy your mind." He keeps talking as his finger pumps in and out of me, sending me into delirium. "… and I'll break your heart."

With that, he steps away from me, leaving me swaying and reeling at his words.

His threat. His promise.

The guilt and anger with which he spat those last words with are evidence that he feels it, too.

There's something between us, and even he can't deny it.

Spinning on my heel, I face him dead on. I straighten

my shoulders, even though my body is still trembling from his touch. "I was destroyed long before you came along, *Master*." I spit the word and stalk past him, but of course, I'm not fast enough.

His grip on my arm is strong, and he pulls me hard against his rigid frame. "Do you want that?" he questions.

"What?" Cocking my head to the side, I regard him in confusion.

"For me to be your master?"

Do I? Yes. *Will he hurt me?* Probably. *Do I still want him?* Yes.

"Tell me," he growls, lifting me by my hips, walking me backward until my body is flush with the wall. His body presses against me painfully, but the pleasure that races through my blood is more than enough to keep my senses heightened.

"Do you want me?" I retort brazenly, which I'm sure will earn me a punishment. The strange thing is, I want it. I'm goading him. Teasing the predator inside him and his eyes light with a blue flame as if there's metal burning behind them, unlike anything I've ever seen.

He doesn't respond, instead, he leans in and whispers his lips over the nape of my neck. Inhaling deeply, he groans and moves his face so we're mere inches apart.

"I want to fuck you so hard, so deep, and so fucking raw that there'll be no other man in your memory besides me. I want to whip you, tie you up, and hurt you, just so I can make you feel good after. I want to see you cry, so I can lick your tears from those beautiful cheeks. And I want to see your deliciously, sweet blood drip from your creamy, delicate skin. And you know what I'll do then?" He doesn't wait for my answer, but continues to grunt each word. "I'll lick that up too and I'll savor your taste because you're mine. You've been mine since I first drove my dick inside your virgin cunt."

My mind is spinning, reeling. My world has possibly tilted off its axis because all I feel, see, and hear is him. He's invaded me. Every part of him has penetrated every part of me. Our bodies are so close it's as if he's trying to mold himself to me.

"Well if you're so tempted to hurt me, claim me, and own me, why don't you? Why am I still just a toy to you? Or are you not man enough to really do something about it?" My sassy retort is met with his questioning glare. It's dark and seductive, just like the man himself.

His hand pins me to the wall, gripping my neck in a vise like hold. "Do not fucking tempt me tonight, little one. You want me, don't you?" he growls.

"Yes." Our gazes are locked in what can only be called a silent war because even though no words are spoken, there are emotions flying back and forth between us like daggers, or better yet, silver-tipped arrows.

"Get ready for work," he says finally and steps back, allowing the cold air that whooshes around me to cool my heated skin. The desire that swirled between us has turned icy, and the heated gaze that pinned me only moments ago is replaced with an indifferent stare. It's as if he's trying to hold back. It's been twelve months and it's always like this. I have whiplash from the amount of times I've pulled only for him to push back.

"Of course. Can't wait to go out there and excite them." If he can be an asshole, I can too. Spinning on my heel, I pull my door open and sway my hips as I walk down the hallway towards the booming beat that vibrates the walls of our home.

We all live in the apartments beside the club. I call it that, but it's a large room which is encased between the girl's apartments and the main mansion where our captors live.

A hand on my lower back has me faltering. He leans in. "Don't try to play my game, Angel. You'll lose," he reprimands on a smirk.

"I wasn't playing a game, Sir, I was merely telling you how much I love my job. I mean, what girl wouldn't want rich men attempting to grope her every night? And what girl in their right mind wouldn't want those hungry gazes on her supple flesh while she taunts them by spreading her legs?" I can't say more because we reach the entrance to the club.

His fingers bite into my arm and he pulls me to a stop. "Don't doubt that I'll be there watching you, closely. If you so much as let someone lay a finger on you I'll chop his motherfucking hand off, and you, you'll get whipped so hard on that pert little ass of yours you'll not be able to sit down for a week." Since I've been here, I haven't been taken to the private rooms I've heard horror stories about. The other girls who work those normally return in agony.

I'm only a dancer, but I know soon my time will come and I'll have to go into those darkened rooms where only the vilest of human's dare enter. Men who want things they're not meant to. The taboo, the sick, the dark and filthy, and we're meant to give it to them.

"Yes, boss." I salute him with my other hand and shrug my arm free. Pushing through the entrance, I leave him standing behind me. The lights and loud music encompass me in their familiarity, and I head toward the back of the stage to get ready.

Samael

She's testing me, and I'm so tempted to show her exactly what my ownership of her would entail. Every night I watch her on stage and every night I'm mere moments away from carving men's eyes out of their skulls because of the way they leer at her.

It's been a year, and I've finally shown her who I am. She knows me now. I've revealed my face to her… But more than that, she knows my heart and soul. Even though she hasn't realized it yet. The desire on her sweet face when she finally laid eyes on me was enough to send me spiraling.

Don't fall in love.

My father's words ring in my ears every time I walk into her room.

Yes, she's one of four girls I train, but there's something about this angel that has me by the balls. Since I fucked her and took her innocence, I've craved another feel of her, but I've had to restrain myself. If my father knew he'd have me killed.

I'm his son, but he wouldn't think twice if he realized I had taken one of his highest-earning girls and deflowered her perfection. But there was something inside me that screamed at me, telling me I had to make her mine. And that voice hasn't diminished, it yells at me every damn day and gets louder by the minute.

"Sam." I turn to regard Kandi. She's been working here for about two years and I've fucked her on numerous occasions, but those plump lips of hers that pout at me don't tempt me anymore.

As the thought settles over me, I realize I have a way to play Angel at her own game.

I step up to the bar as she places my signature drink in front of me—a neat double shot of twelve-year-old Macallan.

"How's work, K?" I question while sipping my drink and she shrugs. Her dark eyes are trained on my lips.

"You know, same old. Men wanting to touch my tits." Her words are meant to taunt, but they don't. The music changes, and I know the woman I really want is about to step up onto the stage and fuck with me. Lyrics hit me, and when I glance at her my heart stutters.

The Weeknd singing "Angel" guts me as she struts onto the stage dressed in all white lingerie.

The little brat changed backstage.

The soft lace panties just about cover her, but I know what they hide. Her corset hugs her curves, molding to her breasts and I have to work at swallowing the whiskey that's stuck in my throat.

The white-feathered wings attached to her back have me imagining how much I'd love to fuck her with them on. Her long blonde hair hangs over each shoulder and covers each of her perfect tits. My cock throbs, and is about to fight it's way out of my slacks when she twirls and I notice she's not wearing those boy shorts she loves, she's wearing a fucking thong that has her perfectly supple ass teasing me. *Christ.* She's trying to goad me and it's working. She must have borrowed that outfit from one of the girls because when I left her, she was in proper panties. Ones that cover what's mine.

The little tease. Jesus her ass needs to be whipped so hard. Her body twirls, bends and it's only when she kneels, and her gaze lands on me, that I know she's intentionally taunting me. Her legs slide open and I'm so fucking hard, I'm about to come.

Reaching for Kandi, I pull her over. Her face is inches from mine, but my eyes are locked on Angel as I press my lips to the woman before me. The irritation, jealousy, and anger that flit over my sweet little angel on stage set my blood boiling.

That's when she shocks the shit out of me by spinning on her knees, getting on all fours, and spreading her legs for the crowd. The men whistle and shout at her and it's enough. My heart rate skyrockets, and all I see is red.

Pushing Kandi away from me, I stalk to the stage. Jumping onto the podium, I pull Angel, and her wings, to her feet and drag her off the stage while getting booed by her fans. Lifting her by the waist, I throw her over my shoulder, and she screeches, "What the fuck are you doing?" She continues to rage, but I don't stop. There's no fucking way I can, because all I see is her bound while my leather whip gets to meet that pretty ass she wants to flaunt. "Hey! You can't—"

Her words are cut off when we reach my wing, and I push open my door. Lowering her to her feet without thought, she stumbles into the room and I slam the door so hard it sounds around us like the bass of a song.

She spins toward me and glares daggers. "Are you out of your ever loving mind?!" Her shouting at me is cute, but it's going to have to stop, because she's pissed me off.

"You want to be fucking owned? Do you? You want me? Is that what your little show was?" Stalking toward her, I watch her back up until she's flush with the bookshelf that covers one whole wall of my bedroom.

"Fuck you." The retort is spat like a venomous poison, which has me gripping her shoulders and pinning her against the wooden shelves.

"You're going to, but not before I show you what punishment means if you want to be mine," I hiss in her face, not missing the tremble of her body.

Her wiggling, trying to get out of my grasp only serves to turn me on more. I've never craved a woman like I do her. It's maddening. "Let me go," she commands, and that has me chuckling.

"Not a fucking chance, Angel." Pulling her along, I push open the door to my playroom. The Dungeon. There are things in here I'm aching to use on her, all in due time.

I tug her over to the bondage bench which has restraints just waiting for her little body. "Kneel." I point to the black leather knee stirrups.

"What if I don't?" she bites back angrily.

"Then I'll make you. Do not force my hand." Her green eyes widen and she shrugs out of her wings. Watching her kneel over the bench is enough to make my blood burn, turning to lava for her. I proceed to tie her legs down, then make quick work of her hands.

She's kneeling, her front plastered to the main section of the plush leather, with her hands and feet bound. Her beautiful ass and bare pussy are waiting for me. "What are you doing?" she questions, and I notice the anger has dissipated. Her tone is now filled with apprehension.

"I'm giving you a taste of what it would be like to be mine." Her gasp has me chuckling. Stalking over to the multitude of whips hanging from the wall and pick out my favorite black leather cat-o-nine tails, which I know won't hurt as bad as the cane. "Now, did you enjoy flashing what's mine to those fuckers?"

"Please, I didn't—"

Before she can beg, I raise my hand and bring down the leather onto her creamy ass. "That's one. Count with me, baby." Her cry is loud sending my desire into orbit.

"One." It's only a murmur, but it will do. For now. "Two." Her counts get louder and I continue. "Three." She's sobbing, but I don't relent.

I rain another lash, and another, until I hear her begging through the haze of desire. Her beautiful pale skin is red and marred with my mark. *Ten. Only ten.*

I drop the whip and crouch at the front of the bench so we're face to face. "Tell me, Angel, did you want to taunt me? Or did you want their filthy leers on your body?" Tears stream down her face and I know her ass must be stinging from the ten lashings.

"I… Please… I just…" Watching her sob because of me rips my heart in two, but also makes me want to fuck her hard and deep. To claim her. Own her fully. But I know I'll never be able to. Not with everything that's hanging over me. "I didn't…"

"You didn't what?"

Teary green pools meet mine. "I just wanted you to see me." For the second time tonight this girl shocks me speechless. *What does she mean? Who else would I see?* She drops her gaze and I feel desolate without her looking at me.

"Angel," I murmur and wait till she meets my gaze again. Reaching up, I allow the back of my knuckles to graze the smooth skin of her cheek. "You're all I've ever seen." My raspy confession stills us both, and the silence hangs thick in the air.

Don't fall in love.

My father's warning lingers in my mind, and I push up, stalking around to the back of the bench. "I'm going to fuck you now." I undo the bindings and pull her over to a sofa I keep in the corner. "Kneel." Gesturing to it, I wait, watching her. I grab the tube of cream, snapping the lid open. I drizzle the cream on the reddened globes of her ass and massage them gently.

I can't have her forever. He'll never allow it. But I can

enjoy her tonight.

The thought guts me, but I pull the thong down her hips and thighs. She turns to regard me over her shoulder as I push my slacks down to my thighs along with my boxer briefs. "Sir?" she questions, and when I lock my gaze with hers, there are too many unspoken words hanging in the air between us.

I reach for her pussy and find her soaked. "Don't look at me. This is just a fuck." And with that, I slam into her tight heat. She's wet. *She's fucking wet for me.* Anger, desire, confusion, and affection coil deep in my gut as I slam into her, and she takes me. She accepts every brutal thrust with loud moans. "Samael," I grit through the agony of holding on to my sanity because she's taking it, all of it, and I know I'll have nothing left once we're done.

"What?"

"My fucking name. Scream it," I command, and as my sweet angel always does, she obeys. We're connected so deeply I feel my soul fuse with hers and I know I'll never be able to break free from it. Her tight pussy clamps down on my dick and I bury myself balls deep. "Come for me, Angel."

Her body pulses, and I reach for her clit. Rolling and tweaking it between my fingers, I feel her come apart. I growl out my release as the anger and frustration of our situation hits me all at once.

Where I Belong

When our souls unite,
Our hearts become one,
Even when you make me bleed,
I know where I belong,
With all pain, comes misery,
But with love, comes agony.

Angel

three years later

"Get up."

The familiar tone that's like a drug startles me awake. His piercing eyes are like the ocean, but filled with frustration and I realize there's something terribly wrong. I push off the bed and fall to my knees like he taught me to.

His wolf mask which covers half his face makes him even more alluring and I realize with him wearing that, it means it's work. I've seen his beautiful face before, but every time he enters my room covered, it's time for me to suffer.

I've finally been taken to the private rooms. The first night there, I was hurt so badly I couldn't work for three days. Sam raged. I've seen him angry, but when he saw the state I was in it was as if the devil himself had taken over his body.

My eyes are trained to the floor and my hands are twined behind me. He loves me like this because he says my tits look good. I've been here for four years and he's never left my side. Yes, I dance for men, and I recently started fucking them. That's what I've been forced into. But this man, who loves to make me bleed, is the one who holds my heart.

"Who's here?" I question quietly, knowing that it could get me an ass whipping. He doesn't like when I talk to him at work. It's against the rules. The rules that we've lived with all this time.

"Be quiet." A growl tells me I need to obey. My body is still aching from when he took me yesterday. We had one hour before his father came home and we didn't waste it. The memory sends a tingle down my spine and the leather of the crop he's carrying strokes my bare skin. All the girls have rooms, we don't want for anything, but there's an underlying current of *disobey and you die* that we all understand.

A fist tangles in my long blonde hair and he pulls me to my feet. At six foot, he's tall and lean with tightly packed muscle. The dark suit he is wearing conceals the solid physique beneath, but I know it's there, which only makes him sexier to me.

You see, this is the man who trained me. He was my first—and even though I have my body used every night—I know he'll be my last.

He tugs my head back so I'm met with almost midnight

colored eyes. His short-cropped hair is growing and the light dusting of stubble on his jaw makes it obvious that he didn't shave this morning. "Behave, okay? Don't cause a scene. I want you perfect tonight. These fuckers aren't nice people, and I'd like to have you back in one piece." His tone shudders through me, and my heart aches for him. To be with him somewhere else. Anywhere but here, where he orders me around like a dog or where I'm trained to be with men who aren't him.

That's all I am, a pet for them to play with. "Yes, Sir," I murmur. The words always seem to calm him, and those perfect lips quirk at the edge. My teeth bite the inside of my cheek to keep from smiling.

As much as he hurts me and as many times as he's made me cry and bleed, he's also made me accept my new life. I've found a hunger in my heart, it's dark, it's unfamiliar, and it scares me sometimes, but with him, I allow myself to let go. To feel it.

When he takes me, I want it, I crave it.

When he hurts me, I love it, I ask for it.

He's my reason to endure. To survive.

Because I know we'll get out of here and when we do, we'll finally be together.

"Put on the little pink dress. No panties. These guys don't want to waste time. You'll dance, you'll smile, but none of them can touch you—and I mean that. Not one finger gets laid on you, okay?" The determination in his expression is alarming. Yes, I've had clients, but this seems odd, for him to be so demanding about keeping a client happy. Perhaps he knows more than he's telling me.

"Why? Are you going to be jealous?" I know I shouldn't but I taunt him anyway. Fire blazes in those pools where I normally find comfort, but they're now filled with frustration.

"Listen to me, Angel. You are mine," he hisses into my face. "All fucking mine. I'll take you up there to tease those fuckers, but when you come back down to your room and you lay on your pretty little princess bed, you'll finger your cunt and think of me. My mouth. My hands. And my fucking cock. You don't need to deny it, because I've seen you do it." With that, he releases me and walks away, leaving me wet and panting. "I'll be back in ten minutes. Be ready."

With one last glance in the mirror, I take in my appearance. Just like he wanted, a sweet innocent girl. Tonight I'll be with clients and he'll be with someone. I know he fucks other women and even though my heart hurts and aches, I know it's all for show.

If his father were to find out about us, about my feelings for him and his for me, we'd be dead. I'm not his only girl, and that thought cuts like a knife. It hurts more than being locked up, bound and manhandled by men old enough to be my father. Because I know in my heart, I love Samael.

Since the first time he took my innocence he owned me. I've never felt more beautiful or pretty than when his gaze is on me. My skin prickles with the memory of azure orbs piercing me.

My hunter. My Wolfe.

Memories of the first time he took off his mask and showed me his face tumble into my mind. My heart stopped, my breathing stuttered, and my body tensed. Those first few months I thought he was a monster, but when I looked into those ice-blue pools I had a completely different reaction than what I thought I would.

He looked like an angel, but he was the devil. And I'd gladly walk into hell with him.

"Are you ready, pet?" The name signals the time has come for me to perform. He's in role as my Master and I obey. I glance at him and take in the poised, polished, perfection that is Samael Wolfe. The Cartier suit that hugs his body is immaculate. Every time my eyes drift to him, I know he feels me because his jaw ticks. It's only slight, but I see it. I know I affect him the same way he does me and it makes me smile. "Don't."

Sucking my bottom lip into my mouth, I drag my eyes straight ahead. "Yes, Sir," I whisper again as we descend the sweeping staircase and make our way toward the east wing of the mansion. It's a sprawling house with grounds that could fit a small city.

"Tonight, after work, I want to take you somewhere, dress warm. I'd like to show you something." His tone is low and the words slowly wash over me like the waves of the ocean. Everything about him is dark, even his name. Samael, the archangel of death and collector of souls. He named me when I first arrived. He called me Angel, even though it's not my real name. I can't tell him who I really am. We're a match made in heaven, or hell, depending on how you look at it. Dark and light. Good and bad.

"I'll be ready." I respond quietly as we enter through the thick metal door and into the main area of the club. It's dark with blue and green strobe lights shining on the girls. The hallway that leads off toward the rooms is dimly lit and he doesn't allow me time to stop and see who's working tonight. Seems I'm heading straight for the slaughter. I count the doors as I always do, it keeps my mind off what's to come. *One, two, three, four.* But we stop at five and I realize this isn't the normal room I'm always in. They're all themed. Each with its own sadistic toys and apparatus. "I'm in here?"

I know the question will go unanswered, but my voice cracks and my heart races. I feel a lump form in my throat. Sam doesn't look at me. He reaches for the door and twists the handle. As soon as it swings open, we step inside and find it empty.

He tugs me forward and stops at the chest of drawers in the corner. Pulling out a leash and collar, he proceeds to fasten it around my neck. Then, leading me over to the four metal cuffs chained against the one concrete wall, he continues silently to fasten my legs and arms.

My body is alert, but not in the way Sam always has it humming with desire. This time, it's alight with fear. "Sam, Sir, why here? You said—" He straightens and gives me a dark look, halting my words. *Plans changed, little one.* It's written all over his face.

"You're going to entertain two of my father's friends." He declares with distinct agony in his voice. When his cobalt eyes meet mine, it's clear as day, he's telling me to be strong and that's when the fear threatens to strangle me.

It's going to hurt, they'll make you cry, but I'm here.

His promise, his vow, his pledge. Four long years and I've been through every moment with him. Each client, every man, all the agony and he always tells me the same thing. Promises me that he'll be there at the end. And he always is. The only problem is that this time he looks stoic. His face is filled with thunder. Those normally sensually curved lips are thinned into a severe line. Dark brows are furrowed above eyes that are filled with defeat. As if the thought of what these men will want to do to me is putting him through the same pain I'm about to feel. That thought scares me more than the toys that are lying on the cabinet beside my bound body.

"Sam, I'll be okay." I offer with a smile, but I know it doesn't reach my eyes and the way he's looking at me tells me my lie doesn't go unnoticed. Before he can say anything more, the door opens and two men walk in with dark masks covering half their faces, they're dressed in suits that probably cost more than anything I've ever owned. Both with graying hair, I would guess they're in their late forties, probably early fifties and my heart sinks. It drops to the floor in front of me like a lead weight and when I drag my gaze back to the man I love, I notice pools shimmering with emotion.

He's apologizing in the only way he can—with regret in his gaze and constriction in his jaw. His body radiates with anger, but he doesn't show it. As if he's been sculpted from stone and there's no chipping away at it.

I'm sure he's been doing this for so long that he finds it easy to hide behind a mask. Behind the mask of the wolf. But I can't, and when I stare at him one last time before he leaves me, I tell him everything I want to say with one look, and I hope it pierces his heart as he does mine.

Samael

I'm not apologetic when I talk to her. I'm not sweet and loving when I fuck her. But I'll be the man she spends her life with.

I taught her.

I made her.

I created the seductress she's become.

Nothing will take me away from her. Not this business, not our clients, and definitely not my father. These two assholes will use her tonight, and there's nothing I can do about it. But it won't be for long. I'll save her from this life. I just hope it won't be too late.

My need for blood is rife. To take my anger out on someone. "Sammy, pretty little thing you got here." The old sick fuck who my father calls a friend steps up to Angel and trails his finger down her bound arm. She's trembling and it takes all my restraint not to lose my shit.

"Yeah, I'm heading out. You two enjoy your time with her." I don't look at her again, I can't bring myself to see the anger, pain, and sadness in her gaze.

We're not a couple. We don't go on dates. There isn't anything I've promised her besides getting her out of here and even that I'm not sure I can do, but I'll die trying.

When I reach the door, I pull it open and step outside the stifling room. This isn't me. I need to lose myself in a little toy tonight. It's just sex, that's what my life has been ever since I can remember. As I pass the rooms, I head into the main area and stop at the bar. Kandi steps up to me. "The usual?" she questions, and I glance her way, taking in the tight black tank top she's wearing.

"Yeah, whiskey, neat. Make it a triple." She nods, knowing not to question me further. All my staff, and yes, I refer to them as mine because my father has given me free reign of the club, know that when I'm in this mood, they are not to disobey.

She sets the glass down and watches me intently. Her eyes bore into me, the heat of her glare stifling. She's been working for me for almost four years. We're not friends, but she's been trained by me. She loves pain, and tonight, I think I'll make her my toy. "You need something?" she questions, tipping her head to the side with curiosity. I glance at the brunette again and nod. Without a word, she pulls off her apron and sets it on the back bar. "Let's go."

Five foot six of pure feisty woman with round hips and a beautiful ass. Her tits aren't big, just a handful, but I love making them hurt. Clamping her taut pink nipples while twisting them until she screams is one of my favorite things to do. We reach the door of room number eight and I unlock it with my keycard. This is my room. Private from the ones reserved for clients, and I've decked it out just the way I want.

The king-size four-poster bed with raven-colored sheets sits against one wall. There are windows that overlook the main downstairs area and from here I can see women gyrating to the music that thumps through the speakers. My toys are packed neatly against the wall adjacent to the bed and there's a large screen above a fireplace, which has most channels, including our own personal porn channel. Yes, we've got cameras in every room, so I can watch Angel being mauled by men while I fuck someone else.

She knows I do it. There are no secrets between us. I'm an asshole and I don't make promises I can't keep, so as much as I want her, to be with her, I can't. We're forbidden and this is how I'm going to survive, by losing myself in another woman while watching the one I want get spanked, hurt, and fucked by others.

"What room is she in?" Kandi knows why we're here, and she's not one to ask more than she needs to know. I respect her for that.

"Five."

"Okay." She smiles, but I don't return the gesture, as soon as she hits the button, the picture appears on screen and I'm riveted. Her face is still immaculate, no tears. One of the men has a flogger and he's using it on her legs, thighs, and I watch intrigued when he gets to her sweet, little cunt.

"Undress, Kandi," I order. It's not her real name, but in this business, it's better to stay in the dark about certain things. Dragging my gaze away from the images that have me hard as rock, I watch the brunette kneel on the floor as she's been taught.

Her breasts are larger than Angel's, and her body is curvier. I grab the cuffs and bind her hands behind her back. Fisting her hair, I tug her up to standing position and circle her while the sounds play out on the surrounding speakers. The yelping of the woman who's burrowed herself inside the cage that holds my heart has the cold rock that beats only for her twisting in agony. "Spread your legs." She obeys and I quickly fasten a spreader bar on either ankle, holding her open for me.

I place one hand between her shoulder blades and push her forward, bending her at the waist. Glancing down, I take in the voluptuous ass that's begging to be marked. Without a word, I grab my whip and trail it between the smooth globes, sending a shudder through her. "You're in the mood for pain?" Her murmured question is uncalled for.

I don't offer a response. Instead, I lift the leather and bring it down on her creamy skin. A red welt darkens and I smile. Yes, I'm a sadistic bastard. I lash her with another and another. All the while listening to Angel beg and plead with them to stop. My arm is aching from the exertion and my shirt sticks to my sweat-laden skin. After twenty strikes I drop the whip and breathlessly stare at the marks I created.

Hastily, I unbutton my shirt and allow it to fall to the

floor. Making quick work of my slacks, I push them down and grip my thick cock. I'm so hard that it's engorged and painful. A peek at the screen has me groaning. The slim form of the girl I tied up for them is limp, but they haven't stopped. Her nipples and clit are clamped and her head lolls forward. I know she's either passed out from the pain, or she's trying to regroup. No matter what it is, I know I'm going to lose my shit right now.

Kneeling, I unlock the spreader bar and with a tight grip on Kandi's hips, I walk her toward the bed. Her breasts plastered to the soft mattress, and her cunt waiting for me. I make quick work of sheathing my erection and grip the toy I'm about to use on her.

She doesn't know what I have planned which is part of the fun. The mirror that hangs above my headboard reflects the angelic woman on screen, and with her in sight, I slam into Kandi deep and hard. Her screams echo around me and my growl is feral, animalistic. Her body accepts every inch, but before she has time to think, I plunge the plastic cock inside her puckered hole without any lubricant.

The cries that escape her are like fuel, driving me, igniting me, making me smile. I don't stop when she begs me to, I don't slow when she lifts her head and I see the tears streaming down her face. This will be the last time I'm with her. I know she'll never easily submit to me again. Not that I want her to. There's only one woman I do want.

My hips continue to slam against her, but my eyes are glued to the screen. Cemented on the image of a girl that I trained, that I took, that I want, being choked with a cock deep in her throat.

And as the thoughts of how much I want to claim her as my own scream at me, I continue my violation of Kandi's body. I'm fucking one woman, but my mind, body, and soul are ingrained with another. Watching Angel being taken like a common whore sends me into a fit of rage and I ram into the tight cunt before me. Deeper, harder, and faster.

She's mine.

It should be me.

My woman.

My fucking Angel.

Suddenly my body locks and my vision swirls black as my orgasm rips through me like a violent storm. A fucking hurricane drags me under and all I see is *her*, while I'm spun around in the fierce clutches of agony and pain.

Before I step into room five, I steel myself for what I'm about to find. After Kandi left, I turned off the screen because I couldn't look at the images taunting me anymore. She's been in here for three hours, and as I enter the room I find her passed out.

They've hurt her badly this time, and I'm going to have to talk to Father about giving her at least a week off to heal. Leaning in, I scoop her from the dirty sheets and stalk out of the bedroom. "Sam, is she okay?" I turn to one of the bouncers and nod.

He doesn't need to know. I don't want everyone

talking about her not being able to keep up with sick assholes. Once I'm in the girls' wing, I head straight for her bedroom and shut the door behind me. Laying her on the bed, I make my way into the bathroom quietly and run her a warm, scented bubble bath.

My mind is running rampant on how I can get her out of here, but with my father keeping such a close eye on everything I'm going to have to outsmart him somehow. When he's not here, the two guards on stand by are, and I wouldn't be able to break her out without bringing attention to myself.

As the steam heats the room, I shut off the taps and head back into the bedroom to find her awake, peering at me from under those dark lashes.

Trust overflows from her piercing gaze that leaves me breathless.

I can't love her.

I can't want her.

But I'm fucked because she owns me.

"What happened?" She questions with a soft moan. When she rolls over, the wince on her beautiful face has me rushing to her side. "It hurts." She mumbles and I nod in understanding.

"It will. I need you to be strong for me, okay?" Reaching up, I stroke her cheek. Her smooth skin touches mine and an electric current shoots through me straight to my dick.

"Samael, I don't remember—"

"Shhh, please, Angel. Just let me care for you." My plea falls between us like a lead weight. I'm the one who put her here, made her do the shit that's hurt her. All I can do is try to fix her. But her gaze holds so much love, so much emotion that it steals my breath.

"Sam, I—"

"Let's get you cleaned up. You need to sleep." For the second time tonight, I scoop her up and head into the bathroom. The moment her skin touches the water a whimper tumbles from her lips. "It's okay, I'm here." Lowering her into the bath, I grab the cloth and soap.

Her body trembles and I know it's in fear. Pain and agony shoot through me, as I wash her skin with gentle strokes. I watch the blood taint the water with its deep red color. The sins of the devils who defiled my girl wash away until I see Angel—her sweetness, her beauty, and her light—shine through.

"You interrupted me earlier." Her murmur drags my gaze to hers. Orbs that shimmer like rare jewels hold me hostage, and I want to hear the words she wanted to say.

I crave them more than anything.

I ache and hunger for them, but it's not the right time.

"Soon, my pet. Soon." She nods and allows me to continue washing her until her skin is glistening and smooth again. The cuts and bruises will heal, but I know the scar on her soul may be there forever.

Angel

"Listen to me, Angel." He regards me with beautiful Cobalt eyes that hold me hostage. "We can never be together. Do you understand me? There are people who will take you from me. They'll hurt you and I won't be able to protect you. This"—he gestures in the air between us—"is only for us. We have to be a secret. Okay?" The man who took me when I first arrived a month ago regards me in earnest.

When I take him in, and I mean really look at him, I see his beauty on the outside, but I also see his demons that he so eloquently hides behind a polished veneer.

His face is covered by a mask, but I see beneath it. I recognize the shimmering light he stifles.

I don't know his name or why I'm here, all I know is I'm glad that I've been released from the man who stole me. From the cage I was locked in. Far from the things he used to do to me. It's true what I told this man, this dark angel. I was a virgin, but that only meant I'd never had a man enter me. That doesn't mean I haven't been violated in other ways.

I nod, but don't voice my response to his request. Instead, I ask a question of my own. "Why am I here?" He doesn't answer. He only watches. Like a predator stalking his prey, a hunter, a wolf. And as this dawns on me, I come to the realization that I'll never escape his clutches, because he is my owner now. I am merely a toy to be used by men. A bargaining tool.

My mind ponders this and I realize that somehow in the darkness my life has become, this man before me—in his exquisite suit, the all-knowing smirk, and the hands that are now stroking every inch of my skin—he's the one I belong to.

I'm his pet.

"You're here because I want you to be. I'm going to teach you, train you. I will make you crave me. When I'm done, you'll yearn for my touch, my whip, and my cock."

He reaches up and strokes my face ever so gently. A contrast to the way he fucked me.

"And if I want to leave?" My insolence will earn me a spanking, but I don't care. I need to know what my options are. I have to know if I'll be able to walk away from this.

"You can't. The only way out of this is if you no longer exist." His gaze flickers with agony and I tip my head to the side with curiosity. I'm kneeling before a man who has the ability to snuff me out with a click of his fingers, but when I see the resignation on his face, I realize this isn't him. I mean truly him.

This life, the things he does, it's not because he wants to.

It's because he's forced to.

"Angel, wake up." Low spoken words in my ear rouse

me from the memory, or was it a dream? My eyes flutter open, and I gasp when I'm met with blue pools filled with concern. As soon as I try to move, my body protests and I realize I passed out from the pain they'd inflicted. The images of two men old enough to be my father flash through my mind and the tears come.

As they stream down my cheeks all I can do is allow them to bathe me in their purity. To let them try to absolve the things I've been through. What my body has endured. I know nothing will ever purge me from the crimes committed against me, but I let myself believe.

"Hey, look at me." His hand strokes my wet cheek and I watch him lick the saltiness off his fingers.

He loves my tears.

He tells me so, often.

But this time he's not the one who's wrenched them from me, this time the pain was inflicted by sick men. Vile devils that want me because I look like their daughter. My eyes find his and I nod.

"I'm fine." I try to smile, but I can't. He lifts me and I wince when I feel my skin tear. "Fuck." The word that falls from me is hissed, low and angry, and suddenly I'm lying back.

"I'm sorry. I tried to move you when you were sleeping, but in your slumber you shifted, tossing and turning. What were you dreaming about?" I shake my head. There's no way I'll tell him about my feelings. He doesn't know I love him. He has no clue how much his presence makes all this bearable.

He can never know because we're not meant to be

together. We're forbidden.

"It's fine. Can you leave me alone please?" After a night with client's we normally have a day off, but judging from the ache in my back and legs, I think I'm going to need more than a day. Anger bubbles up from my chest as he stares at me. I can smell her on him. Even though we're not a couple, it hurts. I shouldn't be jealous, I shouldn't let it bother me, but it does. It slices me worse than the cuts from the leather that burn my skin.

"Okay." He spins on his heel and heads to the door, but before he walks out he murmurs. "I'll be back." With his head hung in, what? Shame? Guilt? I don't know and I don't care.

When I do finally respond, he doesn't hear me because he's already down the hallway.

"I love you."

A soft noise startles me and I roll over, opening my eyes to find the room in darkness. My body hurts and my ass stings as I shuffle out of bed. Padding over to my door, I flip the switch and the illumination that comes from my overhead chandelier is blinding.

"I was wondering how long you'd sleep." A rough voice has me starting and when I spin on my heel, I find Samael sitting on my desk. He looks relaxed as his feet dangle, swinging back and forth. I drag my gaze away from him and head into the bathroom to grab a glass. I fill it with cold water and take a long sip, savoring the cool liquid. When I enter the bedroom again, I climb back onto my bed without answering him. "You angry with me, Angel?" he questions with amusement, and I shoot him a death glare, which has him chuckling.

I don't know why I'm angry with him, he's only following orders, but I have no one else to take my frustration out on. For as much of a controlling asshole as he is, he's been good to me. Caring for my wounds and trying to make me more comfortable when the clients are rough.

He's silent for a while before hopping off the desk and stalking over to me. He stops at the foot of my bed. Those blue eyes pierce me like arrows shot directly at my heart. I wish he didn't affect me. Every day that I've been held captive, I've prayed that I wouldn't feel what I do because he wouldn't want me. He couldn't.

Yes, we fuck, and there are times he's gentle, but I know what I am. A slave. Nothing but a pet for him to toy with. To take his pleasure from when he needs it. As submissive as I've become with him, I still fight. I show him that he can take want he wants from my body, but he'll never take my soul. Even though I know that's a lie too because he's already got it—it's fused to his, making us one.

"Are you going to act like a child?" When he crosses his arms in front of his chest and pins me with a glare, I fight the urge to smile.

"What do you want, *Sir*?" I spit the word at him and fire blazes in his eyes. There's something about me calling him that—it seems to turn him into an animal.

"Sweetheart, do not fuck with me tonight." He growls, low and rough, and it turns my insides molten. I shrug and pull the comforter up to cover my bare legs. He dressed me in a sheer nightdress earlier and my nipples are sensitive against the material.

"Why? Aren't you going to whip me? Add to the slashes on my ass?" The retort comes out unbidden, cheekily, and anger flares in those hypnotic pools. Before I have time to react, he's beside my bed with his hand around my throat. He lifts me easily, pinning me against the headboard, his body cocooning me, and I savor the heat emanating from him.

"Is this what you want?" he hisses. "Is it, pet?" he spits the name he knows I hate. "So pretty, but you know what? You're not pure anymore. And it's not because of what they've done to you. It's because of me." His other hand cups my pussy through the thin material of my panties and I feel his fingers push aside the cotton and enter me. "I fucked you. I own this little cunt. It's mine." He muses as his hold around my throat tightens and as sick as I think he is right now, my pussy pulses and I know he can feel how wet I am. "You see, Angel, you love my hands on you. Your cunt is soaked for me. Only me. And you know what? It will always be that way. Because I fucking own you." With those last few words, he releases me and I sputter, gasping for air.

I grip my sheets and turn my angry glare on him. "You want a reaction? Then here it is. Fuck you! Okay? Is that good enough? I hate you and I hate it here and I hate being a toy for sick bastards!" I realize I'm screeching, but

I don't care because my body aches and the skin on my back burns.

Suddenly, I'm in his arms.

I reach up to punch him but he grips both wrists and holds them behind my back.

"If you stop doing that and acting like a child, I'll talk to you. But if you insist on this display of immaturity, I'm going to leave you here and you can sulk on your own."

"Fine. Then fucking get away from me." He doesn't argue, instead he steps back and allows me to breathe. When he's close to me I lose my mind, my anger, and I need to keep my guard up because one day I'm going to lose it and tell him how I really feel.

"Will you behave?" he questions with a smirk. It's sexy and infuriates me, but I nod. "Good girl."

Two words and he disarms me.

Completely and utterly.

And I'm a docile little kitten.

Samael

She's a fucking tiger, but when I utter those two words she purrs contentedly, which makes my dick stand to attention. "I've asked him to give you a few days off," I utter, dropping my head in shame. Guilt burns through me at what I make her do every day. The agony of seeing her in pain, of seeing her with other men, flays me. It takes everything in me to restrain myself from barging into a room to rip the men off her.

"Thank you." Those two words should never be said to me. I'm not the nice guy and I wish she'd stop fucking with my head. Stop looking at me like I'm her savior. I'm not. I'm her nightmare. I'm the one who took her soul. Took her purity and marred it with darkness.

But as much as I want to walk away, I can't, I want her too much. I'm falling, scrap that, I've already fallen. Deep and fucking fast. I'm in love with her. The thought startles me and I'm rigid with agony.

"Don't thank me. It's part of my job," I growl but don't meet her gaze. I know there'll be pain in her beautiful eyes and I can't bring myself to see it. I'm a coward.

"Are you going to fuck me now?" she questions with that soft voice, and I spin around to find her sitting back watching me with intensity in her green eyes. They're normally the color of tourmaline, but there's always a slight hint of a deep blue that shimmers when she's turned on. I've only ever seen it when I'm with her.

"No. You're in pain. I'm going out tonight." I don't miss the disappointment on her face. I've told her I fuck other women, but I don't. It's a lie I let her believe so she doesn't think I love her. Last night with Kandi was enough to confirm my feelings for Angel. It was the first time I'd indulged in another woman in the four years since I first touched Angel, and before I came I knew it would be the last. Before I plunged deep inside Kandi, I realized it was a mistake. Other women do nothing for me, because my sweet masochist owns me as much as I own her.

Love. Only for her.

"What?" I don't know why I ask, but I do and that pisses me off. She shouldn't have so much control over me.

I'm slipping every day and it's not good. My father will notice it. "Nothing. Have fun." Her murmur is filled with hurt, but it's not physical, it's emotional.

With that, she turns over and covers herself in the thick comforter and I miss those curves that were peeking at me only moments ago.

"I will." She doesn't move, her eyes flutter closed and I see the glistening tears on her lashes. As much as I'd like to go to her, pull her into my arms, and kiss her, I can't.

So I turn and twist the handle on the door.

As she does every fucking time I leave, she mumbles the words thinking I can't hear her.

But I do. I always do.

For years I've wanted to say them back.

But I don't, so I shut the door and walk away.

"Sammy." I turn to find my little sister, Theia, walking out of the room where she's probably been helping one of the girls. She's dressed in a pair of tight black shorts and a bright red tank top. I shake my head and rake my gaze over her.

Her job at Inferno is something she's been glad to have, but every now and then, something brings her back here. I'm not sure what, but she'll return with her light.

"What's up, pup?" She hates the name, but I find comfort in annoying her. Isn't that what big brothers are supposed to do?

"I'm heading out. Dad is in tonight and I'm not in the mood to talk to him. This shit needs to end. I don't know why I come back. Another girl has been hurt and can't work." I regard her through narrowed eyes. She's twenty-five now and after helping the girls for a couple of year, got a job at Inferno, Dax's club.

She's never assisted me with Angel, not because she doesn't want to, but because I don't want anyone other than me with my girl. Especially the night some fucker thought it would be a good idea to whip her on her breasts with a thick leather belt. I almost killed him—it took four bouncers to pull me off him.

"I know, sister. Trust me, there's nothing I want more than all this to end. Once we have the intel we need, it will happen, just biding time."

We walk in silence until Theia asks the question I've been dreading. "You're in love with her. Aren't you?" She doesn't look at me, but the air around us changes and I know she knows. It's a living force between us. My feelings for Angel shifted a long time ago, but I've never let myself voice them. I haven't even let myself admit it to the one person who I trust with my life. My little sister.

We stop outside my office door, but before I can twist the handle, she places a hand on my arm. "Not now, pup," I growl and push the door open. Walking inside, I feel every bit as fucked over as I realize my girl is feeling.

With all that's looming over my head, deep in my heart I know I have to make a choice. She comes first. Her safety. Her happiness. We can't be together in this place, and that means we can't be together at all. Not right now. And that's why tonight I'm ending it. She'll be more without me.

"Don't do this." The warning falls from my sister's lips, but I don't respond. Pulling my phone out of my pocket, I dial the number I should have called years ago. I was just too selfish to admit the woman who holds my heart is better off without me.

I meet her gaze, but don't have time to respond when the man on the other end of the line answers. "What do you want?" He's not friendly. He has no reason to be. But he's the only one I can ask.

"I need your help."

After I swallowed my pride, I showered and headed back to see her. One final time. Time is running out, and I have nothing left to lose. So if one night where I can indulge in her is all I have, I'm gripping it with both hands. As I head down the hallway, I recall my earlier conversation with the only man I knew I could count on.

"What do you want?" His response is everything I knew it would be, harsh, cold, and uncaring. But I have to make him care. I need to force him to see what's in my heart.

"I need your help," I respond, not angrily as I'm sure he's expecting. Instead, even to my ears, I sound as if I'm about to break.

"My help?" he questions in shock, and I nod to myself, to him, to anyone who will listen.

I take a deep breath and tell him the truth. "I'm in love with someone." Words I never expected myself to say startle us both. He's quiet for so long, I think he's hung up on me.

"And what am I supposed to do about it?"

"You have to help us get her out of here, out of Caged." I glance up as I respond. My sister's eyes are wide as she watches me. She of all people should know how difficult this is for me.

"So this girl's done a number on you, hasn't she?" I can almost hear the smirk in his tone and once again, I nod in agreement. Yes, she has.

I push the door open to find her curled up on her bed with a book in her hand. Long blonde hair fans the pillow behind her.

My Angel.

"What do you want?" she snaps before the door closes, and I can't help chuckling.

"To see you." It's one of the most honest things I've ever said to her. All those times I hurt her with my words, it was so she wouldn't fall in love with me. Now, there's no more time to lie or push her away because these are our last few hours alone.

Strolling toward the bed, I settle on the footboard and watch her. With a huff she closes the book and regards me. I reach for the remote at her bedside and turn on the little radio she's got on the cupboard. The song that screams around us from the surrounding speakers has guilt racing through my blood.

"Dance with The Devil" by Breaking Benjamin taunts me. It's a haunting melody, and so apt for this moment. "This is an ominous song." I smile sadly, but my words are far from a joke.

"It is." As the lyrics warn us, telling us to say goodbye, I realize it's the last thing I want to do tonight. I scoot closer to her as he sings about believing in each other and seeing through empty lies. I know everything in my life has brought me to this place. To this moment.

I swipe my thumb along her lower lip and drag my

gaze up to hers. "You're my Angel, and I know you crave the chaos and pain." It's a statement which quirks her lips, tugging on one side of her mouth.

"And you're the demon seeking sanctity within my body every time you take me, Samael," she responds and my heart constricts. I want to tell her I love her. To concur, but I don't. Once again, I drop my hand and turn away from her. The soft sigh behind me is like a foghorn because I know what she wanted. "Are you always going to turn from me? Is my light too much for you?" Her question jars me. *Yes.* I want to tell her. I ache to remind her that I'm death. That being with me or wanting me is not going to bring her love. Straightening my shoulders, I regard her over my shoulder and offer a smirk.

"Darling, if you wanted my darkness I'd know. But you're not ready." My gaze flits to the mirror of her dressing table and I watch her face. She meets my eyes in the reflection and says something that cuts through me like a hot blade slicing through butter.

"I'll shelter you with so much of my light it will eclipse your shadows." I chuckle at her reference.

"You do realize that when an eclipse happens it's the opposite?" I muse, our gazes lock and she grins at me.

"I do, Sir, but I'm sure you're intelligent enough to know what I mean." *That sassy mouth.*

"I do, Angel. Come here." She quickly jumps from the bed and drops to her knees before me. My cock hardens at the sight, but I reach for her and pull her to her feet as I rise along with her.

"Dance with me." I circle my arm around her waist

and grasp her small hand in mine and we sway to the song that's telling me to do what's right.

To say goodbye.

To free her from hell.

"I'll always dance with you," she murmurs, pulling her head back. We stare at each other in a heated standoff, and I see it. All of it. Pure, unaltered love. There's no tension, no fear, just complete trust, and it fucks with my mind.

"I'm the devil, sweetheart. You shouldn't give in so easily," I remind her, but she shakes her head and tilts her chin up in that sassy defiance I've grown to love.

"I haven't had a choice in the matter. I gave in a long time ago." Before she can say anything more I crash my mouth to hers and when her lips part in a soft, dick-hardening gasp I slide my tongue against hers. The sweet whimper is enough to spur me on and I continue to delve into her warm mouth.

She's intoxicating, welcoming, and she's about to leave my life, so I do what I should have done for her first time. I lift her and walk her to the bed. Laying her down, I cover her body with mine and settle between her thighs. "I should walk away," I murmur against her plump lips.

"You should make love to me," she quips, pouting her lips playfully and I lift off her so I can easily tug her panties down her legs. Once they hit the floor, I unbutton my shirt and let it pool behind me. While I push my slacks off, my gaze doesn't leave hers.

"Touch yourself. Show me how much you want me." She spreads her slender legs and her bare pussy is glistening. Her fingers tease her entrance and I watch enraptured as she dips two digits inside her sopping core. *Fucking beautiful.*

Her body bows off the bed and her whimpers come faster and louder. "Stop." Her hand drops to the bed, and she regards me with frustration. "That's my cunt and my orgasm," I order, dropping to my knees and she gasps in surprise.

"What are—"

Before she can continue, I lean in and lap at her beautiful pussy. My tongue darts into her tight heat, and I lick the honey from her body. The delectable flavor heats my blood, ignites a spark in my nerves, and has my body vibrating with need.

I tease her open and take in the pink entrance of her body. "Fuck, you're beautiful." I glance up and she's smirking down at me. "Funny?" I question while pushing one digit into her, pumping it in and out and her body responds by tightening, pulsing around me.

"Please, oh God, Samael, please, Sir." Her begging drives me wild and my Angel grips the sheets while she rides my hand.

"Come for me. Give it to me now." And she does. Every fucking drop of her arousal soaks my fingers and hand and I'm a goner. A man addicted. My face is wet with her sweetness as I rise and hover over her again. "Taste yourself on me, Angel." Our mouths fuse in a heated kiss, and before she can move, I'm sliding inside her.

She's the only person I've ever gone bare with, and it feels like heaven, like we're made to be connected.

All our clients have to use condoms, and all the girls are on birth control, so I know we're safe.

Rolling my hips, I thrust into her. Her legs wrap around my waist and she whimpers into the kiss. We're a frenzy of limbs and sweaty skin. Two bodies fused as one, connected as if we've been joined and can never part. Her hips lift to mine, meeting perfectly, like two fragments of the same piece of glass.

"Oh fuck, please, Sir, Sam." Her words are jumbled, and I feel her tighten around my shaft. My release sends a tingle down my spine, and I know I'm about to explode.

"Whose are you, Angel? Who do you belong to?" The question falls from my lips before I can stop myself. I drive into her relentlessly, stealing her breath and the words I want to hear. "Tell me," I growl against her neck, then lift my head to watch her come apart.

"I'm yours. Always." As she whimpers her promise, her body locks in the most exquisite orgasm I've felt a woman give me. She detonates me like a nuclear fucking bomb and I know wherever we are, we'll always be one.

She'll always be mine.

I'll always be hers.

Angel

"Why are you doing this?" I question the man in the mask, but he doesn't answer me. He stalks back and forth with his stare on me. It's as if his hands are on me, touching every inch of my skin. The heat of the sensation sends my body into overdrive. It's been almost a year and he's never fucked me again.

This is my training. That's what he calls it. He's done everything to me, but never again has he allowed himself inside my body. The ache of having him so close yet so far is unbearable. I shove it down and resign myself to the fact that he only took me because I was still a virgin, but I know it's bullshit.

It's more than that but I'm too afraid to admit it. I'm too freaked out to even imagine what it could mean if I was feeling something for a man who wields a whip and is about to use it on me. My emotions are in turmoil. How can I ache for a man who loves to see me cry? Someone who enjoys seeing me crumble, hearing me beg and whimper. Someone who makes my skin prickle and sting.

"Angel, it's been long enough for you to know why I'm doing this. I've got to make sure you're ready. Soon you'll need to endure much worse." His words hold a promise and I know there are men out there that will hurt me worse than anything he's ever taunted me with.

"I know." The confession is palpable and he stills for a moment. He's always so quiet, a silent predator. Even though my hands are bound and I know I have no way of getting out of the ropes around my wrists, I still tug. Why? Because I want to touch him. I want to see if his body shudders at my gentle touch the way mine trembles at his harsh caress.

"Then don't ask, because you know I can't give you any more than I already have. This is what we are." Cobalt orbs settle on me and in his gaze he implores me. It's as if he's got his hands on me, shaking me, trying to make me understand.

It's not there now. But I always see it—every day when he collects me, something akin to caring. An emotion he doesn't freely give. He hides it behind those cold eyes.

I've still not seen his face, but when he finally reveals himself to me, I'll know. My heart will never be the same. As much as I try to deny it, to tell myself I'm not falling, I know it's a lie. Because deep in my gut, in the soul that I've held onto for all these years, I know when he asks, I'll hand it over to him without remorse.

And as he raises his hand and the soft leather licks against the sensitive skin of my thighs again and again, I realize that I'm not falling. I've already leaped over the edge.

I'm in love with my tormentor.

My heart is his and what he does with it, I have no control over.

I'm utterly owned by him. Every part of me.

"Sir, please?" I beg again, as the realization of what we are turns the lashings he rains down on me into something more.

An entity.

A feeling.

An emotion.

Suddenly, he drops the whip and glares at me. It's a look I've seen before. Desire. My gaze travels down to the prominent erection tenting his slacks, and I want him to fuck me right then and there. Not sweet and loving. Not slow and tender. I want him to give me everything. To do his worst.

I train my gaze back on his and I hope with everything I have that he can read what I'm telling him without words.

"No."

One word. Just one syllable that cracks me wide open. The deep tone of his voice as he denies me the only thing I've ever wanted—the one thing I've craved—sends me reeling into darkness. I shut my eyes tight as I feel the salty emotion trail down my cheeks.

Agony comes to me then, knocking the wind from my lungs and gripping my heart painfully. Heartache is something I've endured, but this is something more. Because it feels as if my heart, that held on for so long, has finally let go. It's stopped, and he's the only one who can make it beat again.

"Why?" Lifting my chin, I try to square my shoulders, but he's got me bound to the St Andrew's Cross. He spins on his heel and saunters toward me with a glint in his eye. When he reaches me, he pushes his body flush with mine, and I feel his erection pressing into my core, right where I need it most. The ache I've

felt since the first time he took me is back and it's burning me alive, lick by ferocious lick.

"Because I'm not allowed to have you. You're my forbidden fruit, Angel, and as much as I crave you, as much as I want to devour every inch of your supple skin, I can't. Even now, as I feel the heat of your body against me, I know that if I took you, if I slid my cock that's rock hard for you, into your beautiful body, our fate will be sealed and we'll both be damned to hell."

He reaches up and strokes my cheek gently, it's the softest touch I've ever felt, but it ignites the yearning, it heats my skin, and it coils the desire deep in my core.

The want that this man wrenches from me makes me crave to relinquish everything to him. I meet his searing gaze head on and I make my vow. "Then I'll walk beside you as we enter through the gates. I'll burn in the fire if it means I have one night with you."

His groan is low and deep and he drops his eyes for a moment as if he's considering what I've just said. Hope blooms like a flower in our dark world and just like that, it's trampled when he regards me again. "I can't tarnish you with my dark, Angel. As much as I want you. As much as I ache for you. I'll hurt you beyond repair." And with that, he spins on his heel and picks up the whip.

"Your words do that more than any lashing you give me," I retort with a strength I didn't realize I had and I see the muscles in his back stiffen under the gray shirt. He glances at me over his shoulder and his lips quirk into a dark smirk. "Don't you see it? Look into my eyes, look at my soul. It bleeds for you." My words are enough for him. I know what he needs.

Without another word he stalks to me with intent and grips my neck, tightening his grasp enough to have my heart flutter and race. It beats wildly against my ribcage as he leans in and runs his nose from my shoulder up to my ear.

The whisper of his lips tickle against the lobe. "You are going to be the death of me. I'm trying to do the right thing," he growls. It's primal, and I realize I've hit the nail on the head. This is my way in.

"I don't want you to do the right thing," I choke out because his grip tightens farther.

Another rumble from his chest vibrates through me. "I'll make you bleed, pretty girl." Those words should instill fear in me, but they do the opposite and have my body reacting with need. My clit thrums. My pussy throbs. My nipples harden further.

"Do your worst," I challenge with a bite and suddenly his other hand rips away the flimsy material that covered my sex, and he plunges two long fingers inside me.

"You're wet?" he grunts and pulls away to meet my eyes. I see the shock in his expression. I try to nod, but I can't because his hand is still firmly secured on my neck. "Fuck." He hisses the word while he continues to drive both digits deep inside me.

"Please?" I beg for release. He's taught me never to come without his permission and my body craves it as he fucks me with his fingers.

"Beg."

"Please, please, Sir. I need to come. Oh God, please." Tears stream down my face as the agony of holding on threatens to break me worse than his whip.

He watches me as he continues his assault. Teasing, taunting, splintering me further. Molding me for him. Only him. "So fucking beautiful. You're exquisite." His words do nothing to diminish the ache, they only intensify my need.

"Fuck... please... I'll... do anything." My words are incoherent and jumbled, but they fall from my lips in any case. My eyes flutter closed as air becomes difficult to find and my body convulses, waiting for the command.

He crooks his fingers against my sweet spot and orders in a gruff tone, "Now. Come for me." And I do.

I shatter. I fly. And then I soar.

My Desolation

The desolation of losing you,
Follows me every day,
The emptiness of your absence,
Grips me every moment,
The memory of your love,
Shatters my beating heart

Angel

"Freya." I glance up to regard the brunette beauty who's making her way to the table. "I'm so sorry I'm late, Dax was fucking around with something, and I couldn't leave." The crimson on her cheeks tells me exactly what happened.

"You mean he didn't untie you from the bed?" I question with an arched brow. She blushes a deeper red and nods quickly.

Blue eyes, ones that are a replica of her brothers', settle on me and she questions, "How are you?" Every time she asks me, I nod and smile. I tell her I'm fine, even though we both know it's a lie. I haven't slept in days. My job is keeping me going, but it's a distraction.

If he knew what I was doing.

He wouldn't care.

The thought dissipates and I glance at her again.

"I'm surviving." It's the most honesty I can give her. Lifting the cup to my lips, I take a long sip of the thick, black tar I've ordered. It's the only way I can get through the day. My nights, on the other hand, those I spend with my favorite men. Johnny and Jack.

When he, along with Kael, Dax and Theia broke me out of Caged, I was given my rucksack with what he wanted me to have and a heartbreaking goodbye. That's all I have left. A broken heart.

Six long months and the pain is as fresh as it was the day I walked out of that hell leaving the man I love, along with my heart, behind. "Frey, baby girl, look at me." Theia's hand rests on mine and drags me back to the present. "He loves you. I know he'll come for you as soon as he can. Don't give up."

She implores me with the same words almost daily. If we don't meet for lunch, I'm normally at their place or she's at mine. She and Dax have been there for me for so long I feel as if we're family. However, I'm not. I'm an outsider. "Did he find out anything?" I question and she nods, pulling a folder from her oversized bag.

"This is all we could find on your parents. It's taken a long time because the guy who helped us was on another case. He says that the information in there may not be something you'd want to read." I nod because I know it isn't.

It's been seven years since I was *taken* and my parents never filed a missing person's report, so what I'm about to uncover will probably break me further. "I can handle it." The lie slips easily from my lips. A soft sigh from my friend stirs the longing in my heart and I glance at her. "Would it be okay if I spend the night with you and D?" I question, and she nods.

"You know you're always welcome, babe. You're family. I consider you the sister I never had." Her smile is as sweet as the woman who gifts it. I've grown to love her dearly. Working at the club, I've become more open to making friends. The other two ladies, Dakota and Skyla are also really sweet. One sexy, little brunette, the other a fiery redhead.

Dax and Theia have always been open to all of us being around, but slowly they've become *more.* I've seen it with my own eyes. Like I did with him, with the man I can't seem to forget. My heart aches, it burns in agony when I think of him, or even when his name crosses my mind. It might seem childish, but he's very much ingrained in me. My heart, my mind, and my soul.

"Just to relax. I can't…" Shaking my head, I gulp the last of my coffee and meet her waiting stare. "I just don't want to be alone." She nods in understanding and rises from the chair, still observing me.

"Come over any time you want, darling. Promise me." I acknowledge her and when she pulls me into a hug, I can't help but feel the ache of emptiness that's encapsulated my heart.

"Thank you," I whisper as she hugs me tight to her slim figure.

"Always."

That's what I told him that last time. I should have known it was goodbye. He was gentle, he made love to me and it was the most beautiful thing I've ever felt.

Throughout your life, you'll fuck people, men and women, but there's only ever one who'll make love to you. And when they do, that's when you crack open. Your heart is ripped from the cage of your chest and it's given to the person connected to you.

As beautiful and perfect as it is, there's always the chance that the person can take it and crush it.

They can break you and you'll live in agony for eternity.

They might be the one, your soul mate, but they may never be meant for you, and that's what you need to be wary of.

Because that... hurts like a motherfucker. As I head home, the memory of the first time Sam made me cry and bleed permeates through me like a drug.

"You'll learn, Angel, to kneel when I enter. And when I demand something of you, you'll obey," he instructs with the command of a teacher, but with the desire lacing his tone of someone who's definitely not here to school me.

He's here to find his release, and I'm the vessel.

My training started two days ago.

The first day he explained what's expected of me.

The second he showed me the instruments he'd be using for my training.

Today is my third day and now I'm sitting on his bed, waiting for my command. The room he's brought me into is decorated in dark hues and an ornate bed, to which I'll soon be shackled.

"Sir?" The word falls effortlessly from my lips and he turns to regard me. "Are you going to hurt me?" It's stupid, but for some reason, I don't think he would. However, this man has too much control and I fear the day he loses it.

"I'll always hurt you, Angel. But, I'll also pleasure you more than you've ever thought possible."

It's a vow.

A promise.

An illicit oath.

He reaches for me then and the simple touch of his fingertips along my skin has my body trembling beneath his command. "How do pleasure and pain come together?" It may be childish to ask a man like him something like that, but I do it anyway. Perhaps he can teach me what real pleasure is.

"On your knees, so I can train your mouth first. It has too many questions." Hungry eyes hold mine in a searing gaze. I'm at his feet, kneeling like the submissive I am.

Silence crowds us and before I can respond, the speakers come alive and I recognize Aaron Richards singing "Monster" and as it haunts us through the speakers, when the lyrics scream through the room, every word tells me there's something here, between us. An entity growing, magnetizing, connecting us.

Perhaps I'm reading too much into it, but the way he's regarding me is so much more. Too much emotion. "You're going to learn to swallow my dick, Angel. Ready?" He doesn't wait, but pushes his slacks down and the thick, angry erection juts toward me with intent to show me exactly what he means.

When his hand grips the steel shaft, I nearly pass out. It's the most erotic thing I've ever seen. Granted, I was still a virgin when I met him, but when he teases my lips with the crown, I feel myself get wet. "Open that pretty mouth," he commands and I obey.

Easily he slips between my plump lips and as soon as his taste settles on my tongue I groan around his cock. It's a salty sweetness that tingles on my taste buds. He slides into my throat and I feel myself constrict, stifling his advance. "Look at me." My gaze lifts to settle on his intense cobalt stare. "Breathe through your nose. Relax your throat." He continues to instruct me on how to suck his dick, and when I do as he says, a low groan rumbles through his chest. "Fuck yes," he growls as he slips into my throat past my gag reflex.

He continues sliding in and out, fucking my mouth. Taking his pleasure. Throughout it all, I realize I'm wet, needy, and wanting him more than I could ever have imagined.

Walking into my two-bedroom apartment, I glance around and realize I'm alone tonight. Sighing, I stalk to the kitchen and pour a drink. The double whiskey sparkles at me in the dim light. After meeting Theia, I couldn't come straight home. Instead, I headed to the bar on the corner to drown my memories. The images of Sam that haunt me. But nothing can take them away. No amount of alcohol, not even work can take my mind off him. Every time a song plays, or I come across a familiar scent, I'm bombarded with recollections I'd much rather forget.

I swallow a gulp of the alcohol, and it burns its way down. I savor the pain. My phone rings at that moment. Thinking it's Theia, I slide my finger over the screen without looking. "Hello?"

Silence meets me on the other end and I wait, thinking

it's a missed connection. When a beat passes, I hear it. The soft, melodic sound of his breathing. I know it's him. There isn't anyone else who can make the hairs on my arm prickle like he does.

"Sam?" As soon as I utter his name the line goes dead. I pull the phone from my ear and notice the call has been disconnected. It had to be him. I'm sure of it. But I've had a few drinks, maybe I'm drunk. Maybe my mind is playing tricks on me because I want with everything I am for it to be him. For it to be Samael Wolfe on the other end.

Perhaps I'm imagining a life where he loved me too.

But I know it can never be. I just wasn't what he wanted, who he needed. Perhaps one of those many women he fucked while he wasn't with me is beside him in bed right now. The thought has me draining the glass and pouring another steep shot.

As much as I'd like to be with Theia and Dax, or even Sky and Dakota, I know it's best that I stay home. Thankfully, Axe isn't home. I'd rather be alone. To wallow in my self-pity without anyone telling me I'll be okay. Because, to be honest, I don't think I'll ever be okay. My heart is shattered, splintered into the tiniest fragments of us. Of who we were.

I reach for the remote and turn on our song.

"Dance with The Devil" by Breaking Benjamin.

He was my devil, and as many times as I was denied telling him how I really felt, even on our last night together—the night he danced with me—I couldn't tell him. Not because he stopped me, but because I didn't know it was our goodbye.

I had my own dark angel and he was everything I've ever wanted and will ever want. The memories have me refilling my glass just as quickly as I drain it of the golden liquid which allows me temporary solace. I glance at the folder that holds information about my parents, but tonight, that's the last thing I want to know about.

I don't want to learn about how they didn't love me enough to look for me. I'm alone and I'll savor it until Axel gets home and drags me from my depression and tries to make me smile. Or tries to make me happy.

Samael

Slamming the receiver on the desk, I growl in frustration at this fucked up situation. Her voice hasn't changed and the sadness that's laced in her tone is more than I can handle. It's been months, but my love for her hasn't diminished.

I haven't touched another woman, not even the girls I'm training. Yes, I hurt them, whip them, mar their pretty flesh, but that's all I can bring myself to do.

She's gone. And even though I know where she is, I can't go to her. All this shit is almost over, but it's taking too long for my liking.

My door swings open and Dax saunters in like he owns my office. If it weren't for his help with my girl's escape, I'd punch him the fuck out for claiming my sister.

"Hey man," he greets as he slumps into one of the chairs opposite my desk. "Angel isn't going to survive this break-up. As much as we all coddle her, there's a sadness ingrained in her, Samael. There's only so much we can do. We need to hurry the fuck up." His warning frustrates me because there's nothing I can do to hasten my father's decision to allow me access to what I need.

The FBI have confirmed they'll be able to take down Harlan Wolfe, but I need to get the proof they need. There are many of our clients that will go down along with this shithole. This has been a long time coming, and if I could get this done tomorrow, I would.

I've spent too long here, sitting back and waiting. My father doesn't trust easily, and even though I'm his son, he hasn't let me in on all the secrets he hides. Now that I'm practically running the club, he's finally given me access to certain records, but not the one's I want and need to take him down.

As much as I hate Dax, I know that he's the only one who can help me. The filth that lurks in these mansion walls is far from what anyone can imagine.

I've seen my father torture and maim people who double-crossed him. Even though I'm his son, he'll not think twice about doing the same to me.

That's why I can't go to Angel. If he knows about her, there's no telling what he would do.

Once I have my father's safe combination, I can find everything we need to send him and his friends to the hell they deserve. They'll all rot in prison.

Every single one of them, including the infamous Harlan Wolfe.

"I have a meeting with him tomorrow. I'll get what we

need," I assure him with a confidence I don't feel. Dax nods in understanding. I'm risking my life, but I'd do anything for my sister and the woman who's etched inside me.

"Did you call her?" His gaze settles on the phone I've practically got crushed in my hand and I nod. "Theia and I are looking out for her, she's staying strong. With Axel, Dakota, Skyla, and Kael she's got family to care for her. She's even accepted a job." This is news to me. My sister didn't mention it when I spoke to her.

"Where? What is she doing?"

He regards me with a guarded expression and pushes off the chair. "At Inferno. She's working the bar. It keeps her busy and keeps her mind off you. She's good at what she does. Sometimes she even laughs, and enjoys herself with the girls." The words have a hint of pride in them and a spike of jealousy knocks me off kilter.

"Are you looking after her? Because I'll fucking break you if someone touches her. You have two of the most important women in my life in your care, so don't fuck this up." My warning earns me a chuckle.

"Sam, as much as you hate me, I'll never hurt a woman. Unless she asks for it." His mouth quirks again and I'm tempted to wipe the smug grin off his face with my goddamn chair.

"Don't be a dick," I growl out in response.

"Why don't you go to her? Explain what you're doing? She needs you, Sam." He doesn't meet my eyes, and as much as I want to, I can't. It's the same thing I think about every day, but I can't see the pain in her expression for what I did that night. Sending her away was the best thing I could have done for her.

"I can't, I'm not ready yet." I knew I had to seek vengeance for all she's been through. There is nothing that will stop me from avenging the horrors my girl had to face. I'd move heaven and earth to right the wrongs.

"She misses you." His words do more than pierce me. They squeeze the life from me. The breath from my lungs. I've never loved, never cared for anyone and when she swooped into my life with her beauty, her innocence, I was fucked. Right there and then I realized that I was capable of emotion. And I was enraptured by the woman who's now gone.

Even if it was by my hand.

"I miss her," I answer honestly. He regards me then. We've never been friends, being civil with him has been difficult, but this right here, me baring my heart and soul, is something I'll never do again. "Tell her…" I'm not sure what I want her to know.

"You love her? Do I tell her to wait for you? Or do I tell her to move on and be happy?" The truth hurts, because I don't know how long I'm going to be stuck here trying to take my father down. He's shrewd, and it may take an army, one that I don't have. "Do I tell her you've moved on?" Dragging my gaze up, I stare at him and I realize the agony on my face must be evident because he doesn't say anything more. But I can't deny her a future.

"Do what you must," I bite out. "Is there someone else?" I question, but exhale a relieved breath when he shakes his head.

"She's too caught up in you, man. I just wondered

what it is you want her to do. You don't know how long this is going to take and you don't have the fucking balls to see her." His words are harsh, but they're true. I don't have the courage to look into those sparkling green pools again and then have to walk away.

"The next time I stand in front of her I want this shit to be over. I don't want the threat of my father hanging over us anymore. It's been too long, and I'll never put her through that again." He nods, but I can tell he doesn't agree with me. Fuck, I don't agree with me either, but my choice is to keep her safe. If my father finds out where she is, he'll have her killed for leaving.

"I'm heading back." Dax waits, but I say nothing more. "See you tomorrow, man."

"Yeah. Tomorrow." And just like that, I'm alone again. Pushing up off the chair, I head for the cabinet and grab my favorite whiskey. Pouring a double shot, I swirl the amber liquid and watch it trickle down the crystal tumbler.

Flopping into my office chair, I close my eyes and sip the alcohol which burns a path down my throat. The memories of my feisty, submissive Angel invade my mind. She is a contradiction in so many ways. I press the button on my laptop and music fills my darkened office as I close my eyes and remember her.

"Broken" by Seether breaks through my silence and my mind flits back to those memories.

Of her.

My Angel.

"Do you enjoy testing me, Angel?" Her bright eyes find

mine and we stare at each other for so long, but she doesn't respond. Her compliance with clients comes easily, but with me, she challenges me like no other woman has before. I wouldn't want it any other way.

"Yes, Sir," she responds cheekily and I can't help smirking at my beauty.

"And do you like the consequences?" I question and she nods. It's been six months since I fell apart in front of her and took her. I slid into her body again after that first time and it was the most healing moment of my life.

She meets my stare dead on and smirks. "Always." The chaos that surrounded me on a daily basis melted away when she came into my life and here I stand, her Master and she my slave.

"Dance with me," I ask and her mouth quirks into a smile. I'm not romantic, I'm an asshole, but this woman drives me beyond everything I ever thought I was. She rises to her bare feet and waits. Circling my arm around her waist, I pull her to me. Her body fits against mine and we mold together, like flames dancing in the darkness.

As if we'd been made as one, ripped apart violently, then placed separately only to find true happiness when we'd found each other again. "You're not as bad as you want us girls to believe," she states quietly and lays her head on my chest, which in turn sends heat racing through me.

Reaching up, I grip her hair and pull her head back so we're eye to eye. "Never doubt how much I can hurt you, Angel. I'm not a nice man. Never have been, never will be." Leaning in, I whisper my lips over hers. "And don't doubt that I love to make you cry. If you test me, I will."

Her gasp sends a jolt of pleasure to my dick. She squares

her shoulders, her beautiful lips lift, and I know I'm in for a retort. "Then make me cry. Show me pleasure and pain. Give me everything you have, Samael." My name falls from her lips like silk draping over smooth, soft skin. Her challenge is more than words because her body trembles with need.

She's become somewhat of a masochist and it makes me ache for her.

No, our relationship isn't all flowers and sunshine, it's darkness, leather, and pain. But as much as I dole out, she's pushes right back. I step back and reach for her collar, quietly I clip it around her neck and my blood ignites, burning through my veins.

"Kneel," I order and she drops to her knees. "Look at me, Angel." Her eyes lift as the song changes and "Don't Fear the Reaper" by HIM filters around us. "You don't fear me. Do you, pet?" She shakes her head and grins. Naughty little girl. "Good, now show me how much you want me." I gesture to my slacks and her slender fingers fly to the zipper. She makes quick work of getting my erection out. "I'm strict with you. I love to punish you, force you beyond your limits, but once you're exhausted, I'll hold you, care for you, and I'll make sure you're sated, little one."

She smiles as her sweet mouth envelops the crown of my cock. The sight is incredible.

This woman has the power to disarm me, to break me, but she also has the power to grant me salvation.

Her light is a beacon in my darkness, and I can't help but want her. To want to bathe in her innocence, even though I know deep down I'm slowly dragging her into my world. And for the first time in my life, I don't want to dim her flame. I want it to *burn bright. I want her to engulf me in her blaze and scorch me until my darkness lies in ashes at my feet. I know that only then will we be able to be together.*

Angel

"Is my little masochist awake?" I roll over to find Sam sitting on my desk. He seems to love that spot and somehow, when he sits there, he looks so much younger. His grin is wide and it lights up his face.

"I am, Sir," I taunt him by purring the last word and I notice the blaze of fire in his eyes. It's been three years since I was brought to the house. When Dax brought me here and told me to trust my maker, I thought he was full of shit, but Samael looked after me. Even when he's training me, his touch is harsh yet gentle, making me crave more of it.

When he does hurt me, though, my body responds to it, becoming needy and wet. Now he teases me and tells me he's turned me into a masochist. "How are you feeling after last night?" I shrug and push up, pulling the comforter up around me. It's winter and the heating hasn't kicked in yet this morning, so my room is chilly.

"I'm okay, he wasn't as bad as he normally is." Narrowing his gaze, he watches me, but I'm not lying. The masked man who took me last night wasn't as violent as he usually is when he takes me.

I started taking clients eight months ago and even though I can see how much Sam hates it, he's promised me he'll always watch over me. My dark angel.

"My father requested you tonight," he bites out on an angry growl. I've never met the older Wolfe, but from what I hear from the girls, he's the worst of all. "I hate it, Angel. There's no way I can refuse him or he'll know about my feelings for you." His honesty has a flurry of nerves stirring in my belly. After years of wondering what we were, he's finally admitted to having feelings for me, and even though I have a daunting task ahead of me tonight, at least I know the truth.

"I'll survive," I promise, but all he does is shake his head.

"I know you will. It's not that. My father can be…brutal." It pains him, I can see the anguish written on his face. "After my father is with a girl, she's never the same, Angel." He lifts his gaze to me and when his eyes land on mine, I see it.

Screaming at me in the silence.

He's falling too.

As much as I want to say the words, I can't. So in our silent exchange, I tell him I love him too.

"Hey sweetheart, get your ass over here," a deep growl comes from behind me, and I spin to find Axel, our head of security and my best friend, staring at me.

"Axe, are you due for work today?" I frown, and he shakes his head while trailing his gaze over me. There's been tension between us recently. He's wanted me since the moment we met, but I know Dakota cares for him so I can't find it in my heart to lead him on.

I love Sam, I always will and being with anyone else just doesn't feel right. Theia said he'll come for me, but it's been too long without him and I ache.

I cry myself to sleep every night. It isn't the way I should live, but I feel like half a person without him near, without him at all. My other half is still stuck in that house.

"I'm off today, but I came in to check on you. I didn't hear you come home last night." He gives me that crooked grin that has most of the women—and even some guys—falling over themselves to get with Axel, but all I see is my friend.

"I know, I tried to be as quiet as possible, I needed time to think," I tell him with a smile. "It's going to be busy tonight." I shrug, wiping the counter.

"Are you dancing?" he questions and my body goes rigid. Dax has forbidden me to get on stage again, and even though I know it will pay my bills, I can't bring myself to fight him on the topic. Having someone look at me in a lustful way is not something I want.

"No, you know I'm not allowed to and I don't want to," I retort, pulling the glasses off the shelf. I continue to stack them on the counter, getting them ready for our cocktail hour which starts in thirty minutes.

"Because you still love him," he murmurs. Axel knows about Sam and me, and I can't bring myself to answer because sadness threatens to choke me as it always does when anyone mentions him, so I nod. "I'm sorry, sweetheart, I didn't mean to bring him up." My gaze flits to his and I see remorse in his eyes.

"It's fine. Did you want a drink?"

He shakes his head and gives me a smile that doesn't reach his aqua eyes. "No, I need to get something done for Dax. And I'm going to stop by to say hi to Dakota." He reaches into the inner pocket of his leather jacket that hugs him like a second skin and pulls out a small envelope. "I brought you something." Regret, or is it frustration, sets his lips in a grim line and I can't help wonder what it could be.

He sets it on the counter, pushes up and strides away in his nonchalant way. "Hey!" I call after him but he doesn't stop, just offers me a wave and leaves me alone in the bar.

I drag my gaze back to the envelope, which has only my name scrawled on the front and my heart stops. It's his handwriting. Samael.

Quickly, I rip it open and find a small silver card with the Wolfe logo on it. I turn it over and find a number. Racing to the phone behind the bar, I lift the receiver, and with shaky fingers I dial the numbers hoping it connects me to him.

Three rings and the voice on the other end of the line, which is so familiar yet so strange, answers. "Angel." One word and I'm a sobbing mess on the floor. I can't bring myself to say his name because I'm sure if I acknowledge he's real, I'll wake up and it will be a dream. "Baby, please don't cry."

His tone is laced with anguish. Only I know how

much this man is hurting and it's only from the sound of his voice. "S…a…m?" I manage to get his name out in between sobs, and I hear his intake of breath.

"It's me baby, I'm glad that fucker did what I asked. Listen, I can't come to you now, but soon. I've almost got all this shit sorted and I'll come for you. I swear on my life, I'll find you, Angel." Just like that, the line dies and I cry out in the empty bar.

My body is wracked with pain as the sobs take over and grip my heart in their wretched claws threatening to rip it from my chest. Unexpectedly, I feel strong arms lift me and carry me to the office. "Jesus, Freya. I told him not to do this." Dax's voice is deep as he grinds out the words. My eyes meet his and he tries to calm me by offering me a smile. "I want you to go home. You're not working like this. I'll have Axe take you home."

There's no way I can refuse because I can't even form a sentence. So I nod as I curl up on the sofa in his office and cry.

"I came for you." Those perfect lips form the words, but I know it's not real. It never will be.

Shaking my head, I step back and take him in.

"Samael." As soon as I utter his name, he smiles the perfect smile that used to make me blush. "I can't do this anymore. You're not here. You left me. I wanted to be with you and you pushed me away." It's all true. He told me to leave and when I did, I had to figure out how to live without him. I had to look

after myself because he wasn't there to give me forever. Even though he promised me a life, he didn't deliver.

Turning, I take a tentative step away, then another and another. The further I get the more I feel the ache in my chest intensify. The pain of him leaving. Unease settles in my gut like a lead weight. My life is empty.

"Angel, please, don't leave me. I'll come for you. I promise." I don't turn because I don't want to see him. I don't want to look into his eyes and see the agony that reflects my own. And as I leave, I feel him disappear.

My body aches as I curl into the warmth of my bed. The banging in my head is enough to rip me from my dreams. Sam's face haunts me every day. There are times I wonder if I'll ever be whole again. Will I ever know what happiness is, or am I doomed to stay in this abyss of melancholy and loneliness?

I roll over and find the room shrouded in darkness. I should be heading out, having fun like most people my age do, but I can't even bring myself to spend time with the people who've helped me leave the house.

Pushing off the bed, I head into the second bedroom and find everything still quiet, so I pad over to the kitchen and fill a glass with water and pop two painkillers, hoping it will ease the throbbing pain from so many tears.

Walking over to the terrace, I stare outside, taking in the darkness of the early morning. The stars are still twinkling in the inky sky and the moon is just a sliver shimmering like a beacon. A light in the darkness. It's starting to get cold and as winter comes, I realize it will soon be a year since I've been free. But deep inside, my freedom means nothing because he's not here.

I turn away and head back into the bedroom. The silence can be deafening at times and that's when I miss my old room. The intricate patterns that adorned the ceiling, the soft pillow that I used to rest on after a night with clients, but most of all the soft thrum of his heartbeat when I fell asleep on his chest.

Sam used to tell me it only started beating when he saw me. Even in the worst situation we had found solace in each other. My eyes flutter closed, but a vibration beside me has them snapping open.

The phone on my nightstand vibrates again and I reach for it, sliding my finger over the screen I voice with confidence, "I know it's you." The soft sigh on the other end tells me I'm right in my assumption. "Please, talk to me," I beg. He always wanted me to beg, and here I am obeying his wishes without him having to order me.

"I shouldn't be doing this." Regret is thick in his voice and I realize he's putting me in danger. Most of all, he's putting himself at risk of being caught.

"I know," I answer honestly and another sigh comes through the phone. "Are you okay?" I murmur my question.

"No, Angel. I can never be okay without you in my life. You should know that." He's frustrated and it's rolling off of his words, causing me to tremble. "When I'm not with you it feels as if my soul has been ripped out. I told you that night, Angel, when you walked out that door, you took my heart along with you, and I won't have it back until you're in my arms again."

My breathing hitches in the dark and my body reacts in the only way it can. The throb between my thighs aches and everything below my belly button tightens. "Sam." His name whispered in the dark, swirls around me, and I hear him groan.

"Jesus, Angel, hearing you moan my name like that… It does things to me. It makes me want to do filthy, dirty things to you." The dark promise sends another jolt to my clit, my nipples harden, and I settle on the bed. Lying back, I listen to his deep breaths.

"Tell me, Sam… please?" Squeezing my thighs together to ease the ache, I wait.

"Slide your hand down your stomach, slowly. Feel your fingers tease their way down. Imagine it's my hand, my thick fingers slipping inside those tiny panties and finding your sweet, wet cunt," he growls, and I obey. My hand taunts me as it moves meticulously down my body to where I need it the most. When I finally slip my hand into the panties I'm wearing, I let out a soft moan.

I am more than wet. I'm drenched.

"Now, I want you to flick that tiny clit. Imagine it's my tongue. Tweak it, tug it, baby. Imagine you're sitting on my face because I commanded you to. I've got your nipples clamped and your collar tightened around that beautiful, slender neck." A rumble comes through the line, I hear his belt buckle clink and I realize he's taking his cock out. The one thing I need inside me.

A moan escapes my lips as he continues to tease me with his words. That elusive orgasm I've chased for so many lonely nights is about to hit me full force, and I'm not sure I can handle it.

"Sir, I need you."

Another deep groan from him and he continues with his filthy promises. "Fuck, Angel, I'm so hard. You don't know what you do to me, little one," he growls. "I'm dying to bend you over and drive into that hot little cunt. Mine. Do you hear me? You are mine. Every inch of your gorgeous body and that incredible mind. I swear to you, when I lay my hands on you again I'm going to fuck you so hard, so deep, so fucking dirty you're going to be molded for only my cock. Those tight slick walls of your body will crave me, like I crave you. I'm going to fucking own you, Angel. I'm going to come to you, claim you, and I'm going to ruin you." Those final few words send me over and I'm spiraling. My toes curl into the sheet as my fingers fly over my clit, dipping into my core, drenched in my release as I whimper and moan into the phone.

"Fuck." The word comes out as a low hiss. My high slowly dissipates and I hear him growl as he comes moments later. It's been so long that we both found our release too quickly and sadness washes over me when I realize we'll have to say goodbye and I don't know when I'll get the chance to talk to him again.

"Good girl. Now go to sleep." And with that he hangs up leaving me sated, yet in agonizing pain. Rolling over, I clutch the phone like a lifeline hoping it will bring him to me.

Even though I know this is for the best, it doesn't ease the throbbing in my chest and it doesn't heal my wounded heart. So I close my eyes as the tears slowly ease their way from my eyes and make their way down my cheeks. As sleep overtakes me, my body still quivering for the man I love, I know deep down he's fighting for me. *For us.*

Samael

It's been two days since I came all over my stomach listening to her over the phone. Forty-eight fucking torturous hours of imagining how beautiful she looked coming apart. Her body unraveling at only my words.

I need to fast forward this whole thing because it's killing me not being near her. Today's meeting with my father needs to yield results. My bedroom door flies open and Kandi comes stalking in.

"What the fuck are you doing?" I growl out, but she ignores me and drops to her knees. "I asked you a fucking question." Her gaze lifts and tears shimmer in her eyes.

"I need your help. I'd never come to you if it wasn't important." My gaze hardens into a stare and I nod for her to continue. "Your father…he's got my son." Her words settle on my heart and hatred sparks every nerve in my body. This has gone far enough.

"Don't worry, I'll sort it out. Did he say why? Is there a reason he's done this?" She shakes her head but the tears streaming down her cheeks tell me she's hiding something. "Jesus, K, you need to talk to me. I can't help you if you're going to hide shit from me." Suddenly, she tumbles onto the bed and burrows herself into a little ball in my arms.

"What the hell is going on here?" I glance up to find Dax glaring at me.

"My father has her son, but I don't know why."

He narrows his eyes as he takes in my shirtless torso. "And she decided that your bed is the best place to be?" The retort has my blood boiling.

"Don't fucking go there, you know I love Angel." The woman in my arms lifts her head and stares at me. Emotion dances across her face and I know she's hiding something. "Kandi, what the fuck are you not telling me?" That's when I see it, the answer swimming in her eyes. *She fucked him.* Gripping her neck, I squeeze, cutting off her air supply.

"Sam, fuck man, Samael, let her loose." My arm is ripped from her, and she falls to the ground sucking in air. "What the fuck is wrong with you, man?" His deep voice booms through my bedroom.

"Tell me, Kandi? Did you want to climb the ranks? You want to be a fucking whore, too?" I spit the words at the woman I've been with on numerous occasions and she never once told me.

"I… He made me… I just—"

"Get the fuck out."

"Please, Sam, I need help. It's my son!" she cries out,

but I'm done listening to her shit. I push off the bed and stalk toward her scrambling figure.

"And it's my fucking brother isn't it?!" I roar back at her. With that, I lift her by the arm and drag her to the door. Once she's outside, I slam it behind me and turn to regard Dax. "She was fucking my father. Did you know?" He shakes his head. There's no more explanation needed so I head to the bathroom and turn on the shower. "I have a meeting with him in an hour. I'll call you after," I tell him through the open door.

"I'll be waiting," comes his reply, and then I'm left alone with my thoughts of what just happened. I have a half brother. Stepping into the warm spray, I steady myself by placing my hands on the tiles. As I drop my head, my eyes close. My muscles are taut with exhaustion and stress. If only I can get into my father's safe, I can get all the evidence needed to finally put him away. Once it's done, I can finally go to Angel and make her mine.

I don't know how long I stand in the shower, but when the water runs cold, I turn off the taps and step out, toweling myself off. I take in my appearance. There are dark circles under my eyes, but the blue is as bright as ever. One day I want a baby with Angel, with blue eyes and her blonde hair. A perfect child.

I've never wanted a family. Not wanting to bring offspring into the world with the Wolfe name, but deep down an innate and primal need begs me to do it, to see her pregnant with my child. For her body to accept my seed and watch her belly grow.

Shaking my head, I head into the bedroom and pull

out a shirt and slacks. Inhaling a deep breath, I get dressed, ready to face the head of the household.

Moments later, I'm heading toward my father's office. As soon as I enter, I find it dimly lit, reminding me of the darkness that surrounds this house, the club and everyone in it, including me. He lifts his head to regard me as I close the door and I make my way further into the cavernous room, settling into a chair opposite his large mahogany desk.

"Samael, what can I do for you, son?" he questions, the word *son* on his lips making me sick. I don't want to be his son. Not now, not ever.

"I think I should be made manager," I speak confidently, "since I'm running the club, surely I'll need access to the records?" I question him in earnest, hoping he doesn't see through my shit. I need to gather as much evidence as I can, but I can only do that if he gives me access to the safe where all the records of clients and financial documents are kept.

He meets my eyes and I wonder how I was ever born into this family. Yes, I'm not a hearts and roses kind of guy. Sure, I enjoy inflicting pain, but since I found Angel, my outlook on life has changed. I'm in love for the first time and I want to own her. Only her, forever.

What we do here has sickened me over the past few years and it needs to end.

As soon as fucking possible.

"Is there a reason you're in such a rush?" His question was something I anticipated, but the shrewd look he pins me with wasn't.

"No, I just wanted to make sure that I'm in line to take over. Since Kael is gone, I figured it would fall to me to carry on the legacy." The shit I'm spewing is enough to make me sick, but when his mouth curves into a smirk filled with pride, I realize he's buying the lie.

"Of course, Samael. You'll be a great leader for what we've built. This is our family's business, your grandfather built it up from nothing." He steeples his fingers and watches me. "You know, I thought that little blonde whore was going to be your downfall." He chuckles and it takes every ounce of my restraint not to dive over this desk and choke him to death with my bare hands.

"She was a toy I trained. Nothing more." The words fall from my mouth, but leave a bitter taste on my tongue.

"Mmm, since she was nothing to you, I'd like you to find her. I've given Dax orders to help you locate her. You'll work together to find the little slut and bring her back here. I'd like to teach her a lesson on respect," he grinds out, and I notice the tick in his jaw.

My hackles raise in shock at this new turn of events. If he finds her he'll kill her. And it will be slow and painful. My heart feels as if it's about to break through my chest when I respond. "Why not let her go? I mean she's replaceable."

"Nobody walks away from me. Your brother fucked up once, I'm not letting that happen again." He likes to remind me of what Kael did. When my brother met the red haired beauty he fell and he fell hard. But that's not what my father means, he's talking about letting his son go and not being able to control him. "Unless you'd like to join him?" He cocks his head to the side and watches me with an intense glare.

"Of course not, father." The tension radiating through me is enough to fuck up my whole plan, but when he sits back and pulls out the paperwork I'd initially come in here for my heart rate calms.

"Make sure the new girls are seen to. I want you focused on finding the little blonde. You and Dax will make a formidable team. Can you handle that?" He pins me with a stern glare once more and I nod.

"You can count on me." I respond, pushing up from the chair, I turn and head for the door. "I'll see you later." Once I'm out of the lion's den, I head back to my office with tension flowing off me in waves.

I can't let him find her. Lifting the receiver, I dial Dax's number, his answer comes within an instant. "What's up?"

"Get in my fucking office now."

I don't have to wait long so I know he was on the property.

As soon as he enters, I bite out the question that was sitting on my tongue like a poison. "You knew he's looking for her?" Silence greets me like a slap to the face. "Why the fuck didn't you tell me?" I grind my teeth angrily, rearing back my fist and slamming it into my desk. "Fuck. If our plan is going to work, you need to be honest with me. I can't walk into shit like that again. It felt like an ambush and I wasn't ready for it."

"I know, I should have told you, but there wasn't time. I know what we can do." Twisting my head, I regard him with a fierce glare. "We need to sit down and talk this through."

At this point, I'd do anything to get this over with, so I nod. "Talk."

We've got everything planned to the smallest fucking detail, but the stress it's putting on me is too much. "Sam." The voice from behind me is tentative and I know she's scared of me. Turning to regard her, I take in the woman who's been fucking me and my father and I feel more disgust for her than I would have if she was a whore.

"Pour me a Scotch, make it a double." She no longer has my respect because someone sick and desperate enough to fuck my father and have his child is nothing to me.

"Please."

"If you can't fucking do your job then leave," I growl out, and she nods swiftly, turning to grab the whisky and tumbler. Placing it on the bar, she pours a large measure and leaves the bottle beside me.

"I wish you luck with Angel."

The name of the woman I love on her lips sends me spiraling. Gripping her throat, I pull her over the bar and hiss in her face, "Do not fucking say her name." Once I've released her, I pick up my glass and down the shot, savoring the burn in my throat as it works its way into my bloodstream.

I pour myself another generous shot and I make my way through the club. One of the girls is up on stage and she twirls to the song, but I don't take note of what's happening. Tonight we set our plan in motion, and I need to stay alert. I down my second shot and head to my office instead of sitting at the bar like I'd prefer to do.

Angel

"*So you're the little whore that's got my son so smitten.*" *The deep baritone of the older man's voice sends a cold shiver over me. I'm in the company of Sam's father and I have to behave tonight because if he learns of our feelings, everything will be over and I'm not sure I'll leave here alive.*

Sam has been tense since he told me yesterday morning that his father asked for me and I don't blame him. My body is trembling with fear, but I keep my eyes on the floor like I've been taught. I met with Harlan yesterday and he didn't do anything, which I thought was strange, but today, he had one of his men bring me to him without his son's knowledge and that's what sets anxiety racing through me. "Look at me, toy." Lifting my gaze, I meet the cold glare of the man who's about to hurt me.

When he leans in, I can't stop the flinch and he notices. A big rough hand comes down on my cheek and the sting of the slap is enough to knock me onto my side. The cold floor sends another bout of shivers through me. "You're just a little slut. Do you think my son will want you?" Spittle flies from his mouth as he grips my hair, pulling me up so we're face to face.

Rage turns his face crimson. "Please." The word tumbles from me without warning and he brings another hand down, gripping my throat. Sam taught me breath play and he's choked me while we've fucked, but this isn't a game, or a scene. This man intends on hurting me.

Air becomes difficult to pull in and my eyes tear up. "You're nothing, you understand me? You will never fuck your way into my family. You're here because you've been acquired for your sweet talents." He sneers and all I see and feel is hatred. He pulls me along, dragging me over to a spanking bench which is similar to the one Sam has in his bedroom.

The old man lifts me like a rag doll and plops me onto the cold leather. He binds my arms and legs swiftly and I find myself on my stomach, my body open to his filthy leer.

"I didn't... I mean—"

Without warning a bite of pain stings my leg, and I twist my head to find the thick leather belt in his hand as it rains down another swat earning him a screech that echoes in my ears. "Shut up! I'm teaching you a lesson, you will obey."

I lose count how many times the leather bites into my skin and I know there's blood. A loud clatter brings me back to the present then I feel cold metal on my body. The vibrations are pressed on my clit and tears stream down my cheeks from the force of the vibrator.

He presses something against my pussy and I know it's another dildo or toy because it's freezing. Suddenly, I'm filled painfully and I cry out again, begging him to stop, but he *doesn't. All I hear is his sadistic chuckle. I shut my eyes so tight I see white behind my lids. Pulling myself in, I try to escape to him, to Sam. Imagining his cobalt eyes burning into me, I see his smile as I'm violated in the tight forbidden entrance of my body.*

Both holes filled and it feels as if I'm being ripped in two. "This is how little whores like you should be treated. Filthy little holes taken because that's what you've been made for. You were the perfect payment." His words wash over me and in my mind I chant the words over and over. Perfect payment... Perfect payment... It's a question, a statement, a truth.

"What do—"

My words are once again cut off by pain searing me. "No questions. I thought my son trained you. It seems Samael has been going soft on you," he hisses in my ear and I realize the sharp pain is a blade slicing through the thin material of my dress. "Such pretty skin. No wonder all my clients want you," he remarks in awe and continues to untie me from my constraints. "On the bed, on your back, legs open." The ache between my thighs screams at me, but I move quickly and efficiently to the bed in the center of the room.

I lie back and close my eyes, going to my safe place. Sam's arms, the way we woke up yesterday when he slept beside me. The warm, safe cocoon of his body calmed my fears as he traced slow circles on my shoulder as he told me stories about life outside the house.

Soon, I'm bound to the corners of the bed. My limbs are pulled taut and every time I move the ropes cut into my wrists and ankles. The drawers get pulled open and then closed beside me and I hear the strike of matches. I'm beyond feeling fear, because there's nothing he can do to me that's worse than I've endured before I came to this house. At least, that's what I think, but I'm wrong, so goddamn wrong.

Heat stings my nipples and trails down my bellybutton to my core. My clit erupts with a boiling sensation and when I finally pry my eyes open I see the hot wax cooling on the most sensitive part of my body. Tears well in my eyes, but I refuse to give this monster more of my tears.

It's then that he leans in, and with his mouth inches from my ear, he vows angrily, "You will cry. If you don't want to do it out of obedience, you'll do it because I force it from your pretty face." The cold tip of the blade presses against my throat as he continues. "You see, men like me and my friends like when you cry. So you'll do it to please us. And you know what, pet," he spits the word with disgust, "when you beg for me to stop, it makes my cock hard. So fucking solid that I stroke it when I think about your pretty body being used. Now, I'm going to see how tight your whore holes are."

Bile burns in my throat at his sick words and I tug again on the restraints, but he's made them too tight and I can't move. "No! Please! No!"

"NO!" Bolting up in bed, the darkness swirls around me and suddenly strong arms circle around me. "Fuck you, get off me!" I screech at my captor, raining punches on his chest, arms, anywhere I can.

"Freya, goddammit, stop." A familiar rumble shatters through the memory. Cracking my eyes, I find Axel staring at me like I've lost my mind. "What the fuck was that?" he whispers, and I realize I must have woken him with my screams.

"Shit." Pushing away, I swing my legs over the bed and attempt to stand.

"Please sit. Let me get you water." He leaves me in bed, and I try to calm myself but nothing can calm me down after the nightmare that's just ripped through me. "Here you go, baby girl." I glance at Axe and offer a nervous smile that I know doesn't reach my eyes. He doesn't say anything more. Instead, he heads over to my sound system and turns on my playlist.

He calls it the *slit my wrists* music. I created it one night after way too many shots of Jack. It's definitely not the happiest music, but it reminds me of him. Samael. "Has he called you again?"

"A couple of nights ago," I respond, my voice croaky from screaming. My throat burns and my eyes prick with tears. As much as I love having Axel here, there's only one man who can change everything. And he's not here. A deep sadness fills my chest and my lungs ache, it feels as if I can't breathe.

It's like being punched in the gut—or being held underwater. That moment when I feel as if my lungs are about to explode from strain. That's how this feels. I don't know when I'll see him again, I don't even know if I'll ever hold him again, feel his touch, taste his lips.

I'm hollow.

People say love is beautiful.

They'll tell you it's life changing.

Yes, it is.

Because my life is over. It's changed me and I no longer know who I am.

I'm half a person. He's gone and I've lost myself too.

"Listen, baby girl, he'll come for you." The reassurances that used to make it okay—that used to make daily survival bearable—don't work anymore.

Dragging my watery gaze to my best friend, I shrug, downing the water he brought like it was alcohol. "I want a drink," I pout and he chuckles shaking his head in amusement.

"You need to sleep. Come on. Let me get you back into bed."

"That's my fucking job." A deep familiar growl comes from the doorway and my mouth drops, my body shudders, and my heart stops. Axel spins on his heel and when he shifts, the figure in my doorway comes into view and sends me spiraling.

"Sam?" His name is a question which tumbles from my lips in a raspy whisper.

"That's me, at least, it was the last time I checked." With shaky arms, I push the blankets off, and dart to the door. As I run up to him, I bound into his strong arms and wrap my legs around his waist. "Hey baby," he whispers into my hair and I feel him inhale my scent.

My Wolfe.

"I'm heading out, Freya." Axel places a tentative hand on my shoulder and I pull away from Sam to nod. "Sam." With that, we're alone and my eyes meet his with a blurry stare.

"You're here." My murmur is raspy with emotion. He nods. Walking me backward to the bed, he lays me down, then hovers over me before settling between my thighs, where he was always meant to be.

"Only for a couple of hours," he whispers over my lips gently as if he's scared he'll break me if he kisses me. His expression is tortured as he regards me with a heated stare, which flits from my hair, to my eyes and over my cheeks, down to my mouth. "You're so beautiful." Another soft murmur over my face as his breath warms me from the top of my head to the tips of my toes. "Angel." A soft kiss. "I'm broken." A two-word confession that stills my heart.

"Sam—"

"I ache, baby," he mumbles as he strokes my cheek with his knuckles. "I've dreamed of you, every fucking night. Every hour of every day that I sit in that place, you're on my mind, in my heart," he growls, but it's not one of his lust-filled ones. This one drips with yearning, anguish, which clutches at my chest. "Angel, you're in my soul." He leans in and places a soft kiss on my lips.

The taste of him is foreign, yet so familiar at the same time. His tongue sweeps into my mouth, and dances with mine in a slow erotic tumble. Sharp teeth bear down on my lower lip when he tugs it between his teeth, biting down hard enough to break the skin, which earns him a soft whimper.

"Jesus, you're so responsive," he growls, licking at the crimson on my lips. "You still taste like my sweetest sin."

"And you like my darkest desire."

With one hand, he reaches down and grips my neck. "You going to be a good girl for me?" Nodding, I watch his pupils dilate, darkening with need.

"Why did you wait so long? You could have come to me earlier." His jaw ticks and I watch him grind his teeth in frustration. I realize I'm asking for a lot. He's trying to keep me safe from his father, but my selfishness wins out and I sound like a whiney teenager. "I'm sorry." Dropping my gaze, I look at the charcoal shirt he's wearing, the top three buttons are undone and the smooth skin of his chest peeks at me.

"Look at me, Angel," he commands and I obey easily, lifting my gaze to his. "I couldn't risk him finding you. Do you understand? It fucking pains me every day not being near you. Just your scent alone awakens my beast and I want to fucking devour you. Not having you beside me is like not having air. But my inability to stay away from you, that ache to hurt you and lick your wounds is too much, so here I am."

His confession has my body humming with need. With an innate hunger that only he can satiate. "Then hurt me, heal me, mark me again," I whimper, lifting my hips to meet his that are settled between my thighs.

"Where's your collar?" he grunts in a rough timbre that rumbles through me.

"In the drawer over there." I point to the cabinet behind him. He rises, unbuttoning his shirt, controlled and methodical, like everything he does. I follow his movements hungrily without blinking. The soft material pools at his feet and the slacks that he's wearing join it.

My Wolfe now stands before me in nothing more than his tight black briefs, sporting a thick erection which has my body pulsing, my core drenched with need. He pads over to the chest of drawers and pulls the top one open, the clink of my collar and leash echo in the darkness around us.

There's always darkness, just once I want us to walk into the light, but until his father is gone, this is where we have to stay. This is the first time since I left that I've laid eyes on him and it's everything I've missed, thought about, needed, and wanted.

"Angel,"—my gaze snaps to his—"get out of your head. I want you here with me." I acquiesce when those pools of desire pin me with a glare.

He saunters over to me oozing confidence and desire. The air around us is electric. "I missed you." My confession tumbles into the space between us. He doesn't respond, instead he proceeds to collar me, tugging the leash forcing me to kneel on the bed for him. I'm wearing a thin silk tank top and shorts and when his eyes drop to my hardened nipples I may as well be naked because the look in his eyes is so feral it's as if my clothing has fallen away under it's scrutiny.

"Did you miss me when you were in Axel's arms?" he growls, tugging again. The collar tightens, and my breathing becomes erratic. "Answer me," he bites out, and the calm control he always possesses slips momentarily, showing me the animal beneath.

"No, he's a friend. I had a nightmare."

My response earns me another basal sound akin to a wild predator. "If he ever, and I mean ever, lays a finger on you, I will slice each fucking filthy digit off his hand." Lifting deep blue orbs to me, his dark gaze holds me hostage and I try nodding, but find it difficult because the leather is wound so tight my breathing has halted.

Suddenly, he releases me, allowing me to fall onto the bed gasping for air. "I know." He's right, I was in the arms of someone else, seeking comfort he couldn't give me because he wasn't here. "You pushed me away." My retort doesn't go unnoticed, when his grip falls to my wrists and he drags me to the edge of the bed.

"On your back, I'll teach that little mouth exactly who owns it. When I walk out of here tonight, every sweet, smooth inch of this body will remember me. It will recall who it belongs to. Open your mouth," he orders harshly, each word laced with desire and lust that drips onto my skin like a balm.

I lie back, my head hanging over the edge, my mouth open. Without another word, he slams into my throat. The sheer size of him has me gagging as the crown of his erection enters my throat. The soft mewls and whimpers that fall from me are unnatural, filled with yearning.

He slides out and back in, over and over again, fucking my mouth like it is his to use. And as I lay there, taking every hard inch, I know it is. I am his.

"Good girl. I own you. You're mine," he bites out through clenched teeth, slamming into my mouth. Tears drip from my eyes, as I choke on his length. As quickly as it started, he pulls out. "On your knees," he barks out and I comply easily.

The cold steel of a blade teases my skin and I glance backward to see him slicing the clothing from my body. "Those were—" A sharp swat on my ass has my words halting abruptly and instead a yelp replaces them.

"No talking." Another two slaps on either cheek have tingles shooting through me, igniting my blood like an inferno. A volcano about to erupt. His hands grip my ass, mauling it. "This body is mine. Your ass, your breasts, and that tight, sweet cunt. You hear me?" I nod in understanding.

I can't see what he's doing, but when I feel it, a loud moan tumbles free and I push back against his face. His tongue licks my slick folds from my clit all the way to my puckered entrance. Again and again, sending me into a frenzy as I take my pleasure from his mouth.

My body quakes and pulses. I'm so close, teetering on the edge of an orgasm so intense, that I'm not sure I'll survive. His fingers drive into my core, in and out, again and again as he fucks me with both digits. I'm dripping onto his hand and his growl is evidence that he wants every drop.

"Good girl, come for me." His order sends me over the edge, barreling through the abyss as my toes curl, my eyes snap shut, and I fist the sheets, crying out his name, over and over again.

Moments, or hours later, I open my eyes and he's above me. Instinctively, my legs wrap around his and I lift my hips. "How long have I been out?" I question.

"Only about three minutes, you seemed to enjoy my mouth on your little cunt." His lips quirk and the sinful grin I've come to love appears. He rolls his hips then, sliding into me easily. "Fuck, still so beautifully tight for my cock."

The slow strokes he teases me with have everything below my belly button tightening. "Please." My plea will go unanswered because this is slow, this isn't a fuck, he's making love to me. For the second time in our relationship, if you can call it that, he's showing me with his body how much he feels.

"Look at me. Watch me worship you." He asks with so much feeling, so much emotion that it slams into me, knocking the breath from my lungs. Our gazes lock and our dark erotic dance moves unhurriedly, the music in the background is haunting as HIM sings "Don't Fear the Reaper" and I don't.

He's mine. The bringer of death is the man I love and I hope he can slay our demons before our time is up because I don't know how much longer I can live without him.

"Get out of your fucking head. Do you want me to fuck you?" Shaking my head, I reach for his face, cupping it gently in my hands and pulling him to me. Our lips meet softly, tentatively, as he kisses me with reverence.

"I want you to make love to me," I mumble against his lips. His cock drives into me as our kiss deepens. Matching his slow strokes, his tongue and erection both fucking me, owning me, making love to me. Our bodies, sweaty with our lust, move in sync as I feel it, the orgasm taunting me. "Please." Another plea and this time he obliges me.

Moving faster, he plunges into my body, faster and deeper. "Come with me." An order I obey easily as my body pulses, squeezing him, pulling him in further and we both fly over the edge in a harmony fit for heaven. Only, I'm afraid we may be going to hell.

Our Salvation

I promised you heaven,
You gave me hell,
I filled you with light,
You gave me your darkness,
In the maelstrom,
Together we find salvation
dani rené

Samael

one year later

"Angel, I need you to trust me. I've got a plan, but I need you to go with Kael and Dax tonight. Theia is waiting at a small apartment for you. She'll help you once you're there." Her eyes meet mine, and I see anger, elation, and fear burning a hole into me as she glares at me.

"What do you mean? You make love to me then push me away?" Shaking my head, I pull her into my arms and savor the fragrance of her sweetness.

"Baby, I need you to go. Get out of this place. I'll come for you, but I want you safe when this place goes down." She stares at me with anger and I know I deserve it. I finally made love to her tonight, I gave her all of me and now I'm telling her to leave without me.

"But, Sam, I can't leave you." I spent the last two hours

inside her, tasting her, touching her and now it's goodbye. I don't have a choice. It's easier with her out of the house. When my brother agreed to help, I knew I had to take the step to save her. He will drive her to the apartment where Theia is waiting. Dax told me he'll be able to get her past the guards, and I agreed without a second thought. Perhaps I did it too late, but I've always been a selfish man. I kept her here for too long.

She's endured enough. "You have to. There's no other way," I implore her, but she shakes her head which frustrates me. I've only got a small time frame to get her out of here before my father returns. "Angel, please, look at me?" When she does the agony in her stare tells me all I need to know. She does love me. Like I love her. But I can't tell her yet or she'll never go.

"Samael," she murmurs, but I shake my head and cup her face in my hands.

"Angel, you're mine. Nothing has changed or will ever change. There's a plan in place and I'd like you safe when it all goes to hell."

She smiles then and my heart soars. "I told you I'd walk through hell with you. Beside you."

"Oh, my sweet Angel. I'd do anything to keep you beside me. For me, please do this. I need you to go with Dax, and I'll come for you. I promise that you'll have the forever you want, but we need to bring all this to an end. I've always been selfish with you, since the first time I laid my eyes on you. You hold my heart, take it with you and know that wherever you go I'll be with you. You'll never be alone." Her gaze glistens with unshed tears, and all I want to do is make her smile.

"So you want me gone?" I didn't think this could be so hard, but her question guts me. She peers up through dark lashes

and her questioning gaze almost has me changing my mind when Dax walks into my office.

"I've prepped everything." I drag my gaze to him and nod. "The car is waiting." His eyes dart between me and Angel and he turns on his heel, leaving us to say goodbye.

"Pet, this is an order. I want you to go now. They'll keep you safe for me till I can come for you." Leaning in, I plant a soft kiss on her full lips. Her tongue darts out tracing my lips as if she's trying to commit me to memory as I am her. Her taste, the feel of her skin and body. That incredible smile, but most of all, her heart.

When we finally pull away, she offers me a smile. "I'll wait for you. For as long as you want, I'll be there, my heart is yours Samael Wolfe."

Dax saunters back in and watches us intently. "Come on, sweetheart. Time to go." And then she's gone. As silently as she walked into my life, she's walked out and I'm left with an ache unlike anything I've ever felt.

"Mr. Wolfe." The voice behind me is tentative and I know why. Pivoting, I meet the dark eyes of my private investigator. "I've got news." The man is almost six feet tall, but when he hands me the envelope, he shrinks back.

Without answering him, I pull the photos from the manila folder, the top one stills my breathing and stops my heart. The beautiful blonde in the photo is smiling and laughing with my sister and Dax. But that's not what angers me. It's the other two people in the photo that have my blood at boiling point.

Taking her in again, closer this time, I notice her face,

her smile.

She's smiling.

The way she used to smile at me.

She's happy.

"What the fuck is Axel Knight doing with her?" I bite out the question, grinding my molars together angrily. Even though I don't want to know, I glance at the man who's brought me the worst news he ever could have. Beady eyes flit between me and the pages I'm holding, but he doesn't answer.

Dropping the pages, I stalk toward him angrily and pin him against the door. "Sir, Mr. Wolfe—"

"I asked you a fucking question. What about the baby?"

"I couldn't get more information, but I think he's only living with them. There's no marriage license, so they can't be married, but my guess is that they're dating." I recall the night a year ago when I was with her and Axel was there in the dead of night. He was there because he's living with her? Anger barrels through me like a storm. My sister and Dax didn't tell me about this and I'm about to lose my shit with my little sister. They sure as hell didn't tell me about a child.

She moved on and had a fucking baby with Axel? How the hell did I not see this happening? We were together only a year ago. Since then, my father had been watching me so closely, I couldn't get away again, I haven't even been able to call her.

"I don't fucking pay you to guess! I pay you to find out what the fuck is going on since my sister decided to withhold information from me and if you can't do that then perhaps I should dispose of you." My growl vibrates through me and my blood boils to the point of agony. *She's happy.* The words ring through me, shattering every ounce of restraint I have. Rearing my fist, I plow it into the wall beside the head of the man who looks like he's just pissed himself.

"Mr. Wolfe, I assure you, I'll find out more information. You need to give me a chance. I've been on the case for two days." His pleading dissipates the crimson behind my eyes, and I nod. Releasing his neck, I step back and swipe my hands over my face in frustration.

This is a fuck up, I've left it for too long and she's moved on. "Find out what you can by seven tomorrow evening. Once you've given me your information, I'll transfer your fee." I turn my back on him and I hear the relieved sigh from behind me.

"Thank you, Sir." The door clicks and I'm alone, detached from everything around me.

Heading back to my desk, I lift the photo of her, taking in every pixel, every tiny box of color that allows me to see the woman I love. Her curves are sensual, the body of a woman who's had a baby. *With another man.*

The sting of my knuckles from punching the wall doesn't match the ache in my chest.

This is ridiculous.

I promised her I'd be back, that I'd be the man she spends her life with. Did the night I risked everything mean nothing to her? I thought she understood why I was doing this.

Guilt, shame, anger, they're all swirling through me like a brewing storm. The hurricane of emotions that send me into turmoil. Angrily I swipe my arm across the desk, shoving everything to the floor with a resounding crash.

"Fuck!" The word hangs in the air, taunting me.

Suddenly, my door flies open and my sister glares at me in frustration.

"What the hell is going on?" Her eyes that match mine flit across the desk, my bloodied hand, and then back to my face. "Sam?" I watch her silently stalk toward me, when she stops beside me, I hand her the photo and hear the gasp from her lips.

"Is she with Axe?" I question, my rage is at an all time high and my fist connects with the desk. "Jesus, Theia, what the fuck are you hiding from me?"

"No." She confesses. Theia drops the photo in front of me and points at the baby who can't be more than a few months old. "This little girl…" Her red fingernail prods at the child. "Is yours." Whipping my head toward her, I regard her with furrowed brows.

"What?"

"Look." She grabs the other photos from the floor and lays them beside each other. Each image shows different angles of the tiny, fair haired child and I take her in. My mind is suddenly racing with questions.

It can't be mine.

"Freya told me about the night you spent with her. When you were meant to be out on an errand for dad. She said you found her in Axel's arms and lost your shit." She whispers like I'm a child who doesn't understand. I nod.

"You didn't want to know about her personal life. I tried to tell you, but you pushed me away. Sammy, this is your daughter."

"But—"

"Samael," when she uses my real name I know she's angry or frustrated with me. "Listen to me. After that night, you told me to watch over her so you could focus on getting the FBI onto dad's case. All these months Dax told you to go to her, he told you that she needed you but you pushed him and me away. I'm your sister and you told me to leave you alone while you deal with this, so I did. Sam, Angel fell pregnant that night and you've got a daughter." Her confession sends me reeling. Too much. This is too fucking much.

"You didn't tell me." I retort angrily. I realize it's not her fault because I asked her not to. Because I couldn't bring myself to look at the woman I let go. Even though it was better that way.

"Sam. Go to her." Dragging my gaze to her, I regard my little sister with apprehension. Fear guts me deeply, but most of all, guilt squeezes my chest making it hard to breathe.

I fall back into my chair and weep. This can't be happening. I have a child. A little girl.

"What if she doesn't want me?" I murmur through my sorrow. The question hangs in the silence between us, and I glance up, waiting for her to give me good news. To tell me that the woman who's held my heart since the first time I saw her still loves me.

"There's only one way to find out, Sammy. And you're

going to have to do it on your own."

My father called a meeting in my office this evening. I'm not sure why, but I have a feeling it's not going to go well. Our plan is at the end. I've collected everything I need. The FBI have requested me to hand in all documentation tomorrow, after that, I'll go to Angel, I'll claim her and my daughter.

The hallways are quiet this early in the morning, but as soon as I step inside my office, I know something is off. Dax is sitting in the chair opposite my desk and my father is standing behind it. "Ah, here he is."

"What's going on?" I question, but when the man I've put all my trust in turns to look at me it feels as if my heart is about to beat it's way out of my chest.

"I've found her." Three fucking words and I'm beside him in a second. This wasn't part of the plan. What the fuck is he doing?

"What?"

"Well, son, it seems you've fucked up this time." The deep rumble of my father's voice echoes through my body. It feels as if I'm standing on a ledge and I'm about to jump.

"I don't know what you're talking about."

"Don't fucking lie to me!" he bellows. "You've been fucking hiding her. Dax here was kind enough to inform me of the pretty little house you've set up for her." Ice fills my veins and I'm about to choke the life out of the man who I allowed into my life when my father continues. "He told me how you got her out of the country. I'll have her brought back tonight."

What he's telling me doesn't make sense. I didn't take Angel out of the country. She's only an hour away from here, that way I could keep an eye on her. My gaze falls on Dax and then the screen of his laptop.

The message, clear as day, screams at me.

Play along.

So I do.

"Father, you can't be serious. She was just a whore." I glance back at the old man and his vile sneer is enough to make me want to throttle him.

"She was. Especially when I used her." My grip on the chair tightens and breathing becomes difficult. The proud grin he gives me is enough to boil my blood. I recall him summoning her, but she never told me he hurt her. I saw her after that night and she was fine, there wasn't a mark on her, which at the time I thought was strange, but I didn't question it. I was just relieved he didn't hurt her.

"What?" The word is out of my mouth before I can stop myself.

"Oh yes, she was lovely. Come here, son, let me show you." He flops into my office chair and turns on the iMac, which sits on my desk. The large screen comes to life, and I stalk around to join him. He clicks the video file, which I notice is on a memory stick, and the video plays full screen.

As soon as Angel appears, my anger skyrockets, sending me into a frenzy. My emotions are like a cup overflowing, but I can't let him see. There's too fucking much. The images on screen are worse than I can ever bring myself to imagine.

Her cries echo through the room and I watch her blood spill. Her body used. Her face contorted in more pain than any of the things I've done to her or the girls in my care.

"She was so talented with that little mouth. Her sweet cunt—" Before he can say anything more my hands instinctively go to his throat and rage propels me. Anger darkens my vision, it swirls around me like a tornado and I realize I'm fucked. I squeeze his throat and even as his hands claw at mine to release him, I don't. I can't. He needs to die. I don't know where the strength comes from, but adrenaline surges through me and I choke the breath from my father.

"Sam, what the fuck are you doing?" Dax's face is pure shock, but I don't care. As the video continues to play, I feel my father's life slowly slip away.

I spin the chair around so I can look into his eyes. Shock is present in his expression as I tighten my hold. Slowly his eyes dim, but before they extinguish completely, I make him one final promise. "You are filth. You are not my father. I swear on my life, this place is over. You are over. I will never be like you." With that, I watch the light fade and then he's gone.

"Jesus Christ, Sam." Thank fuck for Dax because I'm frozen. He turns the video off and pulls out his phone. "Sam's office. Clean up. Now."

And just like that I killed my own father.

Because he was a monster.

Because he hurt the one woman I love.

Because he fucked with the wrong man.

I promised I'd never be like him, and I won't, I'll be worse. I'll make sure all these filthy fuckers have justice served to them on a golden platter.

Around me people move, men rush around, my father's body disappears and all I can do is stare into the night. The darkness I've always had inside me finally took a life.

I killed for her. And if you asked me to do it again, I would. I'd do it every fucking time.

Slowly guilt, anger, and fury grip me in their claws, dragging me under.

"Hey man, drink this." Dax pushes a glass into my hand. Robotically, I down the shot and he refills the glass. "My guys are taking care of it. We'll get the story out that he died of a heart attack or some shit. We've got the medical examiner who'll be more than happy to assist if we keep his name clean." He keeps talking but I don't listen. Nothing stands in my way anymore. I can finally be with her, but I can't bring myself to go there yet.

I'm a murderer.

I've killed.

Even though he deserved it, I've taken a life that wasn't mine to take.

And guilt sits like a lead weight in my chest.

Angel

"Freya, he knows." Shock hits me square in the gut and breathing becomes difficult. *He can't know.* But I can see in her blue eyes that she's telling the truth. I drag my gaze away from Theia's and stare out the window. The sun is coming up on the horizon bathing the room in a soft light, reminding me of what's to come.

It's been a year since that night and I glance at my baby girl in her crib beside my bed. Clueless about how much her world is about to unravel. "Did you tell him?" I question without meeting her gaze.

"No, he had a PI follow you. He's beside himself Freya, he thought the child was Axel's." She chuckles on that last bit of information and I can't help but grin because I know that would have been one hell of a conversation starter.

"Well, he hasn't called, so I guess he's not ready to take on the responsibility." I shrug with anger and sadness gripping me, stealing my breath.

"He will, I know my brother and even though he's a stubborn ass, he's still irrevocably in love with you. There's never been a doubt in my mind that he would find his way back to you." She rises and places a soft kiss on my forehead. "I love you, sis, I know we're not blood, but you're my sister for all intents and purposes. You'll always be."

"Thank you, sweetheart. I'm just ready to go back to work now." She nods quietly, and I know what's coming. She and Dax both want me to stop working at the club, but I can't take Sam's money anymore. I've put it all in a savings account for Layla to use as a college fund. I want her to live the life I never got to have. Not being able to finish my studies is the one thing I am angry about, but since I've been doing part-time classes, I feel as if I can finally have a career.

I've finally moved into the house he bought me because the apartment with a baby became too small. So here I am, waiting.

"How are the classes going?"

Shrugging, I glance at my desk which is piled high with textbooks. "It's okay, I've got so much homework to catch up on. Thankfully I've been able to do it online as well so now I just need to finish my assignments."

"I'm sure you'll kill it, babe. I've got to get to the club to make sure the delivery is handled since Dax is with... Uhm..."

"It's okay to say his name you know. I'm not a fragile doll that's going to break when you mention Sam," I remind her with a small smile.

"I know, I just don't want you to be upset that he's contacted us and… Well, I don't know, I feel like kicking his ass into gear." She shrugs with a grin that only Theia can pull off when talking about something serious like my heart breaking.

"I'll be okay." With that, she leaves me to memories that haunt me as I lie back. The one that hits me is from the night I was so well and truly fucked by Sam, that I felt him for days after. We were rough, both of us devouring the other. For many nights after, I would touch myself remembering how he took me. How he thoroughly claimed me. Not only that night, but all the nights before and after.

I trust he'll come for me. I believe we were destined. And even though my life didn't turn out the way I wanted, I know I was put through hell to find the heaven he's given me.

The metal is cold against my skin, but I know he'll love this. I started dressing for him long before we figured out there was something real between us. The way his hungry gaze trails over my skin every day is enough to set me on fire. This ensemble is new, I've asked Theia to buy it for me and when she brought it to me a few hours ago, I knew tonight would be the perfect night.

I'm scheduled to dance tonight and this will look incredible against the silver backdrop I've asked the guys to set up for me. The choker that clips around my neck is a thin gunmetal leather with three chain links that have thin, beaded metal balls hanging from them in a pattern which covers my breasts. They're strategically placed so they cover my nipples, but I know when I'm dancing they'll shift over my skin and I'll be on display.

Men have seen my breasts before, they've seen my nipples, but I'm not brave enough to bare my pussy, so my panties are a pair of thin silk boy shorts that hug my pert ass cheeks.

"You're not fucking wearing that," a venomous growl announces from behind me and I find the gaze I've been longing for burning a hole into me.

"Why?" Squaring my shoulders, I feel the chains shift and suddenly his gaze turns molten.

"Jesus, Angel, your tits are hanging out." He steps into my bedroom shutting the door behind him. I stifle a giggle because this is what I wanted. They always say never poke a sleeping bear, but I've just gone and woke the beast.

"Don't I look pretty?" I challenge. A deep rumble, almost an animalistic growl, comes from his chest and suddenly I'm slammed against the wall. His hard body pressing me against the cold tiles.

"Pretty? You want to know if you look fucking pretty?" he hisses under his breath. Deep blue pools are dark with frustration and desire swirling like a cloud about to consume me.

"Yes." The response falls like a drop of oil in water, settling on the liquid, not mixing.

I'm taunting him. And I love every second.

"Do you like fucking with my head, little pet?" he growls. "Do you enjoy making me hard as a fucking rock while I watch you sway your little ass for those assholes?" His grip on my arm tightens painfully, but I revel in it, aching for more.

"No, because I don't dance for them, I dance for you." Everything stills at my honesty, our breathing, our hearts, and *the air around us is heavy with emotion. We wait, both watching, like hunters. I break the silence with more foolish words. "I like taunting you, I love feeling your eyes on me. And yes, making you hard as fucking steel is my ultimate goal so you'll come back here and take it out on me."*

His eyes narrow, his tongue darts out to wet his lips and then his mouth crashes down on mine in a soul stealing, all consuming kiss. His tongue darts into my mouth dancing with mine as our breaths become one, our bodies both hungry with need, and our hearts both beating with the same rhythm. My hands come up, and I hold him against me, needing the rough with the soft.

Big, strong hands grip my ass painfully as he squeezes both cheeks, pulling me against his body. The thick hardness of him presses against my core, but nothing he does satiates the ache deep in my belly. Only having him inside me will do that, and I know we don't have time.

As quickly as it started, he breaks the kiss and steps away from me. "Jesus, Angel. We need to go." He scrubs his hand over his head, over the short dark hair that's shaven within an inch of its life.

"Is that it? You treat me like I'm yours, by being jealous over something I'm wearing, but when I allow you in you push me way?" I grind out, biting back the tears threatening to ruin my make up.

"We can't do this now. Let's go." And he closes down again, as always.

Pushing by him, I make my way up the stairs, ignoring him shouting for me. Every time I dance, he does this, and every time I fall for it. I let myself feel for him, well fuck him.

Stalking into the club, I head backstage and almost knock Genie on her ass. "What the hell, girl?"

"Sorry, I'm just pissed off, he's an asshole." She's one of the girls I've gotten friendly with, and she knows about my feelings for Sam, what she doesn't know is that I'm falling in love with him.

Her long black hair swishes as she shakes her head. "You and the boss man must be careful, okay?" I nod, and head into my dressing room to check my make up.

He hasn't followed me, and frankly I don't want him to. No, that's a lie, I do want him to. Theia's voice booms through the thin walls as she announces me. I make my way to the back of the stage and wait for my song to start. I've asked her to play a new song, one he hasn't seen me dance to before. Even after the stupidity in my bedroom moments ago, I still want to do this for him. I still want him to see me.

The song echoes, booms, and vibrates through me as I step on stage. "You're The One That I Want" by Lo-Fang is slow, sexy, and the lyrics are perfect for the message I'm trying to convey.

I twirl, my long blonde hair swirling loose around me. The pole they've put on stage for me glitters and shimmers. As I grip it, I see him at the bar with a tumbler in his hand. With a naughty smirk, I wrap my legs around the metal and do my sexiest dance yet.

As soon as the song ends, I'm back on my feet for my second and last song of the night. "Dirty Little Secret" by Bullet for My Valentine booms around me and my body moves in time with the music. Closing my eyes, I get lost in the song, ignoring the jeers and words being thrown at me from the vile creatures I'm entertaining. There's only one man I want and I can feel his gaze on me like he's right here touching me.

I feel his hands, lips and body as I bend. When I kneel on the stage in the pose he taught me, ass up head down, I can practically feel my skin burning from his glare.

When I open my eyes from where I'm positioned, my gaze lands on his and, in that moment, as the lyrics—"You're an animal"—seem to be talking about us, I smirk and slowly push myself up.

The song ends and I give my audience a curtsy and head off stage to screams for an encore. But I don't go back. I can't. I head to my bedroom. The hallway is dimly lit and I don't hear him behind me until I'm at my door and suddenly I'm propelled forward. "Did you like your little display out there?"

"You mean me doing my job? Yes, it was fun."

"Don't bullshit me, Angel." His anger is palpable, but he has no right to be. This is the life he's given me, so he's got to get over it.

"You have no fucking right to be angry, you also have no fucking right to scream at me for no reason. You've—"

My words are halted when he crashes his mouth on mine. With a tight grip on my hips, he brings my body flush with his and I feel every ridge of his torso. Reaching up, I twine my hands around his neck and hold on for dear life, because there's no other place I'd rather be.

I'm unsteady when he lifts me and allows me to wrap my legs around his waist. "I want to fuck you into next week for your childish display." He growls out in frustration.

"Then why don't you?" I taunt. He walks me toward my dresser and gestures with his chin to the sound system, which I

168

turn on to my playlist for him.

"I'm going to, right now. I'm going to fucking hurt you, my little Angel."

"Good."

"You've turned into a little masochist, baby," he murmurs in awe. Nodding, I grin under his heated stare. It's true. The pain he doles out takes me higher than I ever could have imagined. He reaches for my hand and tugs me to my bed. "Bend over, grip the sheets and hold on tight." I do as he says, then before I have time to think, my panties are ripped away and I'm bare to his gaze.

"Sam—"

"Quiet. Nothing from those pretty lips of yours unless it's you moaning my name." His words send a tingle through me. He kicks my legs apart and I'm now splayed to whatever the hell he has in mind as my punishment.

"So pretty, this pussy is mine. It belongs to me, Angel. You belong to me," he states with confidence, more so than ever before. The feather light touch of his fingers trails its way down my spine to my ass, then slowly, he makes his way to my core.

I'm soaked just from a simple touch.

With both hands, he grips the globes of my ass, opening me in an obscene manner, and devours me. My knees start trembling as my belly tightens, and I feel the orgasm that's about to implode ease its way to my pussy.

"Sam, Sam, oh God." I can't form complete sentences, and the only word that escapes my lips is his name. His fucking name.

The white-knuckle grip I have on the sheets is so tight, I'm sure I'd be able to shred them. "So delicious," he growls behind me, his warm breath fanning over my drenched entrance. "You taste like sin, my Angel."

"Please, Sir, may I come?" I purr in the way I know he likes.

"Not yet. You haven't earned it." He rises, leaving me panting for more. I hear the shuffle and my drawer opening and closing, then my hands are pulled behind my back and my wrists are bound at my lower back. "Up and turn around. I want you on your knees." Obeying the command, I quickly rise and pivot, meeting dark pools of desire. I drop to my knees and open my mouth. "Good girl." No more words are spoken while he pushes his briefs down and strokes his cock for me.

I flick out my tongue and lap at the salty pre cum on the tip, savoring him like he does me. Then he slides into my warm mouth. With my eyes trained on his, I watch his head drop back when I swallow him into my throat. Humming around the crown, making him growl out my name.

This man is utter perfection when he's lost inside me. He grips my hair and starts moving back and forth in my mouth, again and again. When suddenly his body locks and I feel warm jets of release coat my mouth and throat. And I do what any good girl would. I swallow each drop.

When his eyes meet mine again, he grins. "You're perfect. Now you will come." His cock falls from my mouth and he lifts me to my feet. "You ready to come, baby?"

Nodding, I offer him a shy smile. "Yes, please." He reaches behind me and unfastens the rope.

"Hold on tight, Angel, you're going for a ride." I frown in confusion when suddenly, he lifts me up and walks toward the wall. "Ready?" I'm still confused, but nod, then let out a squeal when he lowers, lifting me so my legs are draped over his shoulders, my back flush with the wall, and his face buried

"Samael!" He ignores my cries and eats me like I'm his salvation, redemption, and absolution.

Shaking my head of the memory, I push off the bed when Layla starts screaming. Lifting her, I hold her to my chest and coo in her ear to calm her down. She must feel the tension in me because she doesn't simmer down.

I head to the music player and turn it on. She normally calms down when there's music playing. "Shh, little one, you'll be okay. We'll both have your dad here soon enough. I don't know how he'll take to being a father, but he'll just have to learn, won't he?"

The sun is setting on the horizon and our room is bathed in the deep orange glow. Walking over to the window, I glance outside wishing with everything I have in me that I'll see Sam walking up my drive with nothing but a ring in his hand.

When I find it empty, my heart drops. It's silly. I'm being silly. Glancing down at my baby girl, I notice she's suckling on her thumb. Her big blue eyes are exactly like her father's. "You're just like him aren't you? You're going to give me grief," I tell her earnestly and she coos and giggles.

My heart constricts painfully, but when I remember the night we conceived her, I can't deny it was one of the most beautiful moments I've ever had with him.

I just hope there will be more of those. I pray there will be.

"Sleep now, little one. Daddy will be home soon," I

promise her, but deep in my heart, I don't know if he will. All I can do is hold out hope. And that's what scares me.

Samael

"Man, we need to get into the East Wing where your father kept the safe." I regard Dax and nod. He's right, we need to see what he hid in there, perhaps more evidence, before I head to the FBI tomorrow. The key he found on my father's body is held tight in my fist.

"Let's go." As we head up to the side of the house I've never been to, wariness settles over me and when I turn the key to the double doors which lead into the private wing my father lived in, I'm taken aback. There's a whole other world inside.

The living area is furnished like an elite gentleman's lounge, beautiful, expensive sofas and a pool table. The place is kitted out like it's part of the club, but I've never seen it. As we delve deeper into the space we find a bar with more sofas and then I see it. Three St. Andrew's crosses against the wall, further in are more cuffs, chains, whips and toys against the wall.

"Jesus." Dax's voice grabs my attention and I find him opening drawers of condoms, dildos, clamps. It's like a fucking torture chamber in here. I head out toward the bedroom and find a small office. I know this is the camera room. My father had so many set up around the house to *watch* his girls.

Opening the drawers, I find rows and rows of tapes. Pulling them out, I notice they're each titled. Paige, Freya, Kandi, Brit, Charley, and they just keep going.

"Sam, take a look at this." Pivoting, I head out of the small office and find a door cracked. Pushing it open, I take in the opulent bedroom decorated in creams and pastel colors. It's outfitted like a bedroom for a girl, and bile rises in my throat.

"What the fuck is this?" I step farther inside to find Dax poring over papers, photos. When I join him, I notice each page is titled with a girl's name and the date. He flips through them, one by one, and there are some I recognize and some I don't, when suddenly a blonde beauty snags my attention. "Go back, go back."

He does and there she is. Sitting on the bed before us, her wrists bound to the headboard and her long blonde hair loose in waves. She's naked except for a pair of soft pink panties. *Freya Blythe.*

Jesus, she was only sixteen when she came here. How the fuck did I not know this? Kael was right. My father was always a monster.

Pushing away, I head back into the camera room and pull out the tapes, finding the one's marked Freya, I take the one with a number one on it and pop it into the player. The screen lights up and there's my girl, my woman, my fucking pet. The man who walks in only moments later has my hackles rising. It's not my father—it's a man I thought was dead. The one person I believed was murdered for what he did.

My uncle. Harkin Wolfe.

Twins, Harlan and Harkin Wolfe were well known in the upper class social circles, but when the older brother by five minutes was pronounced dead, we all breathed a sigh of relief. It seems he's alive and well.

Anger boils from deep in my gut. Guilt, confusion, everything hits me at once. I watch them all, tape after godforsaken tape and with each one I feel more pain, more agony, and the fierce need to hold her, to make up for what my father and uncle did.

The fifth one sparks to life and there she is, bent over with the sick bastard I called uncle behind her, when he shifts I realize he's got an anal hook inside her with a rope tugging it every time she moves. She's pleading with him and all I can fucking do is slam my fist into the desk so hard it cracks under the sheer force I hit it with.

"Fuck!" I growl when I see him continue with his assault on her, only he's not fucking her, he's hurting her more than I ever did. More than I ever would. The hot wax he drips on her sensitive areas must be excruciating. Rearing back, I slam my fist into the screen. The pain from the glass slicing my skin doesn't even register because all I see is red. I storm back into the bedroom and tear it apart in a haze of fury.

Ripping paintings, vases, whatever I can find from the cabinets and off the walls. By the time Dax puts a hand on my shoulder, the place looks like a tornado has swept through it.

"Say goodbye, man. We're leaving." With that, I walk out without another look back. We've got all we need, and it's time I claim my woman and give her the vows she needs to hear from me.

"This is the paperwork you need. It took me so long because he never trusted me. When he died, I found the keys, combinations, everything I could to get what you needed." I place the folder with every client's name, address, their kinks and fetishes on the table. The two agents nod. They don't know I killed my own father and they'll never know. They think he had a heart attack, Dax and I covered all our bases so all that's left is to get all the other fuckers arrested.

The folder I've just handed them has every name of all the clients that ever visited and partook in the events at Caged. And as I sit back, watching them pour over the pages, I know I've done the right thing. It's been years coming, but after what happened with Kael, I had to make it right somehow.

"Thank you, Mr. Wolfe. As we said, you'll be acquitted in exchange for a full testimony and access to the mansion with everything as it is now. The girls will be released to a home for abused women and they'll be cared for and assisted in finding jobs, possibly education for those who want to study. They'll have a full life. We want you to remember that as of now, you're no longer an employee of your father or Caged. The money from the estate will be transferred to you—"

"No, I don't want money. I've got what I need to get by, my trust fund which my mother set up for me when I was born has been a nest egg for me. Nothing from that place is mine, it should be divided between the women we freed." He regards me quietly and then nods in understanding.

"We'll need you to stay behind to fill out paperwork and you'll be called in about a month to appear in court. We haven't set a date just yet, but once it's finalized you'll be contacted. Please do not leave the country." He places a thick document and pen in front of me. "You'll need to sign this. Read through it and make sure you understand what's required of you." They both push up and head to the door.

"Thank you," I respond and then I'm alone with my thoughts. Once I sign this, there's only one place I'm going. To see my woman and my child.

The need to hold her has been sheer torture for me. I've missed her in ways I can't myself fathom. Opening the contract, I read through the pages and as I initial them, signing away my rights to anything in that house, I realize how much freedom I'm allowing myself, and the girls.

I wish it didn't take so long for him to trust me. I could have been with Angel sooner than this. Now that the time has come, I'm afraid she won't want me anymore. But she doesn't have a choice. I won't take no for an answer.

Just like all the times we were together. When she submitted to me. She dropped to her knees and relented to my commands, and this time will be no different.

"Angel, you're beautiful," I murmur in her ear, causing a slow tremble to trail down her body. Her skin smells like honey, or perhaps sunlight. "Do you like being trussed up as my little plaything?" I question and she nods. The soft mumble of her voice is stifled by the ball gag in her mouth.

She's wearing my collar, my gag, and she's bound to the large X of my St. Andrew's cross. Her inquisitive nature brought her here and now she's at my mercy. However, that sassy little mouth of hers hasn't earned her leniency, it has, however, earned her an afternoon of delightful torture by my hand.

Lifting the soft leather whip I know she loves so much, I raise it and bring it down on the smooth skin of her creamy thighs. A small red welt rises and I continue her punishment with another swat to her other thigh. Her body craves it and I in turn ache to give it. We may not be an average couple, but the love I have for this woman is unparalleled to anything I've ever felt.

My heart beats for hers. Our souls are entwined as one. "Did you like answering me so rudely before?" I question, dragging my gaze lazily up her thighs, stopping at her pussy, and then continuing the leisurely trail to her face. She shakes her head and moves her mouth, the pink gag between her lips is dripping with saliva and the glistening tears that stream down her face make her more beautiful than anything I've ever laid my eyes on.

Stalking toward her, I grip her chin and lift her head so our eyes are locked. Big green pools pierce me, searing my heart and soul in the process. This sweet, innocent girl has embedded herself into my life, but most of all she's opened my eyes to something more… Something that I could never have begun to understand because of the life I grew up in.

She's given me love.

She's showed me light.

She's taken the heartless monster and turned him into a man.

My body quakes with a sudden need to connect us, to be inside her and absorb her innocence and goodness. I've been cold all my life, but she's bathed me in warmth.

Reaching around, I undo the strap and the pink ball falls from her mouth. "I lo—" I press a finger to her lips to silence the words I ache to hear. This isn't the place for such beautiful sentiments. This dungeon we're in is for the dirty, the dark, and the filthy.

"Not tonight, Angel. I need to fuck you raw. I need to make your body ache. Every inch of you will feel me." With one hand on my slacks, I unzip them and push them down. My cock jumps free, solid and ready to drive into her.

I kneel, undoing the ankle cuffs and when I rise again, I lift both her thighs so they wrap around my waist. Her tight heat is wet. She's drenched for me. Ready to take me inside.

A swift roll of my hips and I'm buried balls deep inside the woman who holds my heart. I may be her Master, but she's the one who owns me. I pull out and drive back in, deeper than before. Her body is molded to me, tightening and squeezing. The sweet honey that drips down my cock is all the evidence I need of how much this woman craves me.

"Fuck me, Sam, please." Her hoarse whisper unravels me,

awakens my inner wolf.

Echoes of her cries and moans bounce off the walls in a symphony of erotic sounds, a sensual song of our bodies uniting, burning, and scorching each other as we climb up the hill to bliss. To the abyss that only we know.

"Come for me, my pet. Wet my dick with that sweet cum. Drench me. Mark me like I'm going to mark you," I growl into her ear and she does. Her mouth finds purchase on my neck and her teeth pierce the skin as I do the same.

Her crimson life force floods my mouth as mine does hers and I know in that moment, we're both well and truly fucked.

We'll both be walking into hell.

Side by side.

The reaper and his mate.

The angel and her devil.

Shaking my head of the memory, I glance around and push the contract away. Every page is signed. All that's left is for me to find her and make her mine once and for all.

To see my little girl and hold her in my arms. My own flesh and blood. Rising, I fasten the buttons of my suit jacket and head toward the large steel door. Pulling it open, I find the hallway bustling with agents. "All set?" Detective Briggs appears at my left.

"Everything is signed. You don't need me for anything else do you? I have somewhere I need to be." He proffers his hand and shakes his head.

"No, we'll let you know about the court date. Other than that you're a free man, Mr. Wolfe." I allow the words to wash over me. I'm free.

"Thank you." As I make my way out of the building and head to my car, my phone buzzes. Pulling it from my jacket pocket, I swipe my finger over the screen and greet my sister. "I'm free." Two words that will mean more to her than anything else I have to say.

"Thank God." Her relief is palpable. "She's at home."

That's all I needed.

"Alone or is Axel with her?"

"Don't make me slap you across the head. She's in love with you, not Axel. So stop acting like a spoiled brat and go get your girl."

She's the only person, besides Angel, that I'll allow to speak to me like that. Slipping into my driver's seat, I start the engine and when it purrs to life, I feel the calm take over me. I'm about to see Angel and needless to say, I'm nervous.

A grown man scared to look into the eyes of a girl. Although, she's not a girl any more. She's the mother of my child and the woman I'm going to spend the rest of my life with.

Pulling out into traffic, I head down toward the place where my heart has been safely stowed away for so long. The drive isn't long, and when I arrive, I park outside and sit back, watching for signs of life in the house.

Everything is quiet until my phone buzzes again. I pull it from my pocket and see Theia's name. Sliding my finger along the screen, I answer, "What's up, pup?"

"Are you just going to sit there in the car?" Her incredulous tone comes through the line and I turn to find a black town car parked not far from where I am.

"What the fuck, Theia, are you following me?"

"I was checking on you. Go after her you big lump."

"You think she wants me banging down her door right now?"

"Of course! She loves you. Any woman would want the man they love to fight for her. Stop being so fucking stubborn, Samael Wolfe. You're a free man, you've wanted that woman for six years, and now is your chance to be not only her husband but a father to your daughter." My sister has this annoying way of always being right. As much as I'd like to sit here and fight her on this and come up with reasons why I shouldn't go after Angel, I don't. I undo my seatbelt and open the car door.

"Fine. Now stop following me, I'm going." I hang up before she can respond and slide out of the driver's seat. This is the house I set up for her.

When I broke her out of the club, I bought a house so I knew she'd always be safe from prying eyes. Now that my father is dead and everything has been shut down, I can finally live my life. I've missed my younger years, but nothing will stop me from making the most out of the second chance I've been given.

She is mine now.

She always has been.

It's time for me to man up.

I lock the car and head to the door. I've never been so nervous before. I feel like a damn teenager. At the light blue door, I push the buzzer and wait with my heart thudding painfully against my ribs.

As soon as the door swings open I come face to face with her big green eyes.

The slave I trained.

The submissive I crave.

And the woman I love.

"Sam."

"Angel."

We stare at each other for so long I feel as if it's a dream. That I'm not really here, and she's going to vanish as soon as I blink. But when I finally do and my eyes open again, she's still standing before me. Her beauty magnified. I'm certain she's gotten more gorgeous since the last time I saw her.

"I guess I should invite you in." She offers a small smile, one that doesn't reach her eyes. Even though I've been around her many times before, this is the first time all threats are gone, and it's just her and me.

We're stepping on unchartered territory.

"Thank you." I step over the threshold, and the smell of food hits my nostrils immediately. "Am I interrupting?" She shakes her head and blonde waves tumble back and forth, making her look nineteen again.

"Let's sit. I'm just finishing up dinner. Layla will be home in an hour." Her words slam me like a punch to the gut, and I meet her gaze. "Our daughter," she says matter-of-factly. Even after all this time apart, the need to punish her for being bratty warms my blood.

"Just because I haven't spanked you in a long time, doesn't mean I don't still want to. Don't doubt that I'll take you across my knee right now." My threat hovers between us, taunting her and the visible tremble that shoots through her is evidence that she's still mine.

"Samael, you cannot come in here and do this. I've waited. I'm still waiting. But enough is enough, you need—"

Stalking to her, my hand grips her throat, and I walk her backward till she's flush with the wall. Her breath catches in her throat. "Is this enough for you? This is what you missed, isn't it? Do you want me to treat you like my slave? Or do you want to hash out our shit before I fuck you?" I lean in so our lips are inches apart. Her sweet breaths are shallow, and I know she's struggling.

"Fine." One word and I release her. "You're such a—" Before she can finish her sentence, I pin her with a warning stare and she nods, pointing at the table. "Sit over there. I need a drink." She's almost lost her training. I'll have to remedy that as soon as I've got her bound. When she returns, her eyes are trained on the floor. "I brought you some water."

She places the glass on the table and settles in the seat opposite me. Her gaze hasn't left her bare feet and I glance down. Her toes are painted with bright pink polish which offsets her creamy skin.

"This is what we've become, Angel." I reach over. My index finger lifts her chin, so that her beautiful gaze meets mine.

I stare into deep green pools.

In them I find myself.

I find my heart and soul.

I take the rest of her in and fully study the woman

she's become. My hungry gaze trails over her, and I feel as if I've been kicked in the gut. I wish I was. Perhaps it would hurt less knowing I hadn't… couldn't be with her for so long.

Her body is beautiful even after child birth. Her long blonde hair is loose down her back in messy waves and she's glowing. Positively exquisite in every sense of the word.

"We've always been this, Sam. You just didn't want to admit it. All these years I waited with baited breath, but I didn't give up. I couldn't let you go, but I also couldn't tell you the words." I nod slowly as I regard the woman who's held my heart for so long, I can't remember a time she wasn't embedded inside me.

"I knew, Angel. I've always seen into your heart." The confession tumbles from my mouth unbidden. My chest hurts as I watch her, she's changed so much, but still there are parts of my Angel, bits of my submissive, my slave. I've missed so much.

"You have, as I've seen into yours. Samael, I've always been able to see your soul. Your demons, your darkness, it was the only thing I knew would help me make it through. You know why?" She pushes up from the chair, but doesn't wait for me to respond. "Because I needed you and what you offered. When you hurt me, I knew it wasn't because—"

"It was," I croak, and when I drag my eyes to hers, I see the resignation in them. "I did want to. I loved your tears and the way you screamed my name. Begging me, pleading with me. And when you gave me what I wanted, then I gave you pleasure. I made you come over and over again. And every moment with you was me satiating my hunger, my addiction. You're my vice, Angel." Conviction laces my tone like a thick malt whiskey, burning its way down my throat.

She places both hands on the table and leans in. I expect her to spit in my face or slap me, anything to make the guilt go away but what she does tell me tilts my whole fucking world on it's axis. "Samael, I know. There've been moments being away from you that I've questioned myself, wondering how on earth I'd come to fall in love with my captor, my tormentor, but I realized it wasn't you. That was your father, he was the one who bought me, you were my savior. My dark angel. The other girls used to talk about how you snuffed out the souls of your pets, but with me, you only made me burn brighter than I ever have before." She stops to take a deep breath and her chest rises and falls along with it.

"Angel—"

She places a finger to my lips and I'm tempted to flick my tongue out to taste her, but I refrain, for now. "The day you took my virginity was the day you owned me. The more I looked into your eyes, I found not the Grim Reaper, but the man hidden under all those layers. All those days and nights we spent together you didn't even notice the change in you, but I did. Things between us shifted, something more tangible than Master and slave happened. We fell in love, Samael. You claim to know me so well. Do you even realize every time you whipped me, my screams weren't of pain, but of pleasure?"

I can't find words to respond, to give her what she wants. Love was never in my plan and then this innocent girl stumbled into my life and now as I regard her, I know she's right. When I don't answer, she spins on her heel and stalks toward the hallway. I'm left alone at the table with my emotions to keep me in check. With the words she's just confessed to reel me in.

I want her, there's no fucking doubt about that. So I push off the chair and follow her down the hallway. It's silent and when I find the master bedroom, she's in the kneeling position on the floor, her collar and leash in her upturned palms and her head dipped.

The soft pink panties she's wearing are the only thing that adorn her perfect body. Her knees are perfectly spread so I can see the juncture between her thighs. With her back straight, her breasts jut out and her soft pink nipples are already hard.

Fucking perfection.

"Angel, look at me," I command, easily falling into the role she's allowing me, even though she doesn't have to. Her gaze lifts and she peers at me with the same innocence that compelled me six years ago to claim her. Crouching before her, I take the collar and proceed to clip it around her neck. "You are mine. Do you understand me?"

"Yes, Sir." Two words and I'm rock fucking hard.

"Good girl, now clasp those hands behind your back like I taught you. Let me see these beautiful breasts." Her obedience is intoxicating. I rise to full height and tug on the leash, "Stand, little one." Having her beside me like this is everything I've wanted since I first laid eyes on her.

With no distractions. No one to tell me I'm not allowed to love her, because I do.

"Where's Layla?"

"At daycare. Theia will pick her up and bring her home." I nod before pulling my phone from my pocket and scrolling to find my sister's number.

"I'm calling her. She'll watch Layla for a little while before bringing her home because I need to get reacquainted with you and your body."

"Yes, Sir." I hit *call* on my sister's name, and she answers on the second ring.

"Did she throw you out already?" she giggles, and I'm ready to tell her to fuck right off, but I need a favor.

"Don't be annoying, pup. I need you to watch my daughter for a little while longer this afternoon. I've got something I have to do and Angel will be indisposed." I don't need to elaborate because my sister knows what I mean.

"Yes, of course. Take your time. I love spending time with my niece."

"Thank you." Hanging up, I regard my blonde kitten again. "Now that that's sorted, I think we need to see how well you remember me. Don't you think, Angel?"

"I'd like that." I round her supple form and rain down a harsh swat on her pert little ass.

"Are you already forgetting your place?" I growl in her ear, reveling in the shiver that shoots through her.

"I'd like that, Sir." She's demure, shy, and exquisite. This is where I'm meant to be. I lead her toward the small white stool of her dresser and let her sit.

"I want you to keep your hands behind your back. Where's your rope?"

"In the closet, top shelf on the right." Dropping the leash, I head into the walk-in closet and find the shelf in question. The crimson silk rope is twined like I taught her, and I wonder if she's used it since she left.

In the bedroom, I take my time intricately weaving the soft strands around her elbows down her arms to her wrists. "Tell me, Angel, did you miss me?" I round the chair and crouch in front of her. Meeting her green eyes that are filled with desire, I wait for my answer.

"Yes, Sir, very much."

"Open your legs. I want to see that gorgeous cunt." Her knees part, and my mouth waters to taste her. But before I do, I need to have her teetering on the edge for me. Reaching into my pocket, I pull out the small knife and when I meet her eyes, I see the trepidation in her gaze. "I'm not going to hurt you."

"I know, Sir."

"Good girl." I trail the sharp steel against the fabric covering what's mine and when it falls away the sight that meets me leaves me breathless. "Angel." Above her pussy, toward her left hip, is a tattoo, it's small, but intricate, an *S* designed with a scythe. The blade of the reaper.

Reaching up, I trace my finger over the ink, and she confesses so confidently it stills my heart. "I'm yours, Sam. I've always been yours."

Angel

He must be in shock because he's quiet for such a long time, I wonder if he's angry. Although I can't see it on his face. Stoic and serious as always. "Yes," he mumbles so quietly I'm not sure I heard him right. He rises to full height, and I watch hungrily as he unbuttons his dress shirt.

He's still as gorgeous as I remember. When I submitted to him moments ago, it wasn't because I was forced to. It was because he does own me.

He's always owned me.

There wasn't a doubt in my mind.

I want us to be a family. And since he's here and not rushing to leave, I realize he hasn't told me what happened to Caged or his father. But I'm not about to ruin our time together and ask, so I sit waiting for whatever he has planned.

The shirt falls to the floor with a soft swish and the hiss of his zipper echoes around us like a melody, taunting and teasing me. Black material pools at his ankles and he easily steps out of his slacks. His socks follow the rest of his clothes until he's standing before me in only his dark boxer briefs that are so tight, the prominent ridge of his erection is obvious.

Instinctively, I lick my lips at the memory of his taste. "You want this, baby?" he questions while stroking himself through the material, and I nod swiftly. "Before I feed you my cock, you need to see something." He turns around, and with his back facing me, he orders calmly, "Eyes up."

I slowly trail my gaze up his thick thighs, over the tight, sexy ass, up to his muscled back and let out a gasp at what greets me. *Holy shit.* His perfect skin is filled with ink. Two angel wings adorn perfectly sculpted shoulder blades with the word ANGEL in prominent script in the middle. "Sam."

"You've always owned me, Angel," he confesses and faces me once more with such adoration in his gaze it paralyzes me. "Since the moment you laid those pretty gemstone eyes on me I was yours. I may be the Master, but you own me as much as I do you. Only once in our time together was I with someone else, and even then, it was you I saw. And when you left, I didn't, couldn't touch another woman. I've always been yours."

I bask in the warmth of his words and let them linger before I take them and allow them to seep into me. Allowing them to bathe me in the security that we're going to be okay. The almost two years without each other has somehow made us stronger.

"I love you, Samael Wolfe." The confession hangs heavy with emotion. It's the first time I've voiced the words and it's the first time he's allowed me to. A small grin cracks his ever present, serious expression and he nods.

"I love you, Angel, I always have. And I promise you that I'll love you until my last breath." He places a hand on each of my knees and pushes my legs apart. Deft fingers stroke my bare pussy and I bite back a whimper. "Fuck you're already soaked," he hisses under his breath, then pulls away and slowly licks my arousal from his fingers. "I've missed your taste, pet."

"I've missed yours." I answer honestly. Suddenly, he rises and pushes down his briefs. The thick, angry erection juts out level with my mouth. He grips it firmly, giving it two long strokes, the pre cum glistening on the tip and he rubs it over my lips. "So pretty with my arousal on you. Open your mouth, baby, I want to feed you my cock." His low, gravelly tone sends a shiver of need through me.

Parting my lips, he pushes into my mouth and I moan around the crown, tasting the salty sweetness of him has my desire in overdrive.

"Ready, Angel?" I try to nod, but I can't because he grips the leash and pulls me forward as my mouth engulfs his length. The tip hits the back of my throat and I swallow every inch as my nose hits his groin. "Jesus, that's it, pet, take my fucking dick." He pulls out and slams back into my throat, over and over again. Saliva drips onto my breasts as I take everything he's giving. "Eyes on me."

Lifting my teary gaze, I meet his molten stare.

He fucks my mouth, owning it and I love every minute. Without warning he pulls out completely and leaves me glaring up at him. "I wanted—"

"You'll get it, be patient, baby." The mix of sweet and dominating is heady and I feel dizzy. His fingers are back at my core, stroking, teasing, and delving into my sopping pussy. My body quivers around his digits, but before I can find my release he stops. "Your body is perfect," he murmurs with reverence as he takes in my new curves, my full breasts. The heat in his hooded gaze is enough to have me throbbing to find my release. His mouth attacks my breasts, suckling my hardened, aching buds, biting down on them till I'm mewling like a kitten.

"Oh, God, Sam, Sir, please?"

He ignores me, continuing to taunt my nipples like they're his favorite candy. Midnight blue eyes peek up at me from between my breasts and his face cracks into a satisfied grin. "I love when you're a begging whimpering mess, my little Angel." His fingers once again tease my pussy, pumping into me, slow and steady. The torturous movement has me bucking my hips against his hand, hoping and praying for some relief. "You're being a naughty girl, pet. Fucking my hand like that,"—he smirks salaciously—"but I enjoy watching you squirm. It makes me hard as fuck."

"Please, Sam, please, I want you. I need you."

He drops his hand and I whimper at the loss of his touch against me, inside me, on me. Rising, he strolls behind me and the rope loosens, when it falls away he massages my arms gently and plants feather light kisses on my skin. "Stand."

He leads me over to the bed and lays me down like a fragile doll. "Sam—"

"Shh, Angel." Silence envelops us and he hovers over me, settling between my thighs. "You ready for me, baby?" I nod and he nudges my entrance, slowly sinking into me, inch by torturous inch and I revel in it. Savoring the way he's claiming me with every roll of his hips, I wrap my legs around his waist to pull him closer.

"Oh, God." The moan falls from my lips and I bring my hands around to grip his shoulders. Digging my nails into his skin, I'm sure I'm drawing blood.

"Good girl, take me, Angel. I'm going to fuck you so deep, until we make another baby." His words still me, and when I meet his lingering gaze, he's smiling.

"You want that?" I whisper in surprise.

"Of course, I do." He thrusts again and again until he's entered me fully. My legs tighten around his taut waist and I dig my heels into his ass, pulling him in deeper until he's hitting *that* spot. He leans in, his mouth hovering over mine, and he whispers over my lips. "I love you, Angel, I fucking love you, forever." My body pulses at the confession and my hips buck. "Come for me, sweetheart. I want to feel you unravel around my dick." And I do. My body locks and every nerve alights with need, desire, hunger and my orgasm splinters through me.

"Fuck!" My head drops back, and I feel his teeth on my neck, biting down. I realize he's drawing blood, and a second release hits me, causing my body to squirt, drenching him in my arousal.

"Jesus fucking Christ, Angel," he growls, and I feel him thicken inside me before jets of hot release fill me like never before.

The room is filled with a comfortable, satiated silence. When I finally come down from my high, I feel Sam slip out of me and he settles beside me. Wrapping his arms around me, he pulls me against him, planting a soft kiss on the top of my head.

His skin glistens with a sheen of sweat and I lean in to lave at his nipple savoring the saltiness of my man. "You're so fucking perfect, baby," he coos and I smile up at him.

"So are you," I respond with a smile as he traces circles on my back with his fingertips and I shiver.

"Angel." My name tumbles from his lips and I peer up at him. "I need to ask you something." His serious tone has me on edge. After the emotional afternoon, I'm not sure I can take anything serious because I may just crumble. But what he asks me makes me smile from ear to ear. "I want to collar you permanently. I want everyone to know you're mine. I want to put a ring on your finger, too, but I want you, our daughter, and hopefully another little one. I want a family, Angel. With you."

I stare at him, taking in every word, each promise, and the love shining in those beautiful eyes. I nod, slowly, but excitedly. "Yes, I'll be yours. I don't have a choice, anyway. You've had me since day one. Not only my body, but my heart and soul," I respond contentedly.

"Good girl," he growls and I purr against his side, burrowing further into his arms, enjoying the warmth he seems to emanate.

Once again silence surrounds us, but it isn't uncomfortable, it's filled with ease, the tension we grew so accustomed to is gone.

A knock on the door echoes down the hallway and I shoot up, scurrying around, I pull on a pair of sweats and a T-shirt, "You're beautiful." Sam's words halt me suddenly and I turn to observe him slowly pushing off the bed. "It's Theia, don't rush." He pulls on his slacks and shirt, encircling an arm around my waist, tugging me along with him as we head into the living room to find Layla and her aunt.

"Did you two kiss and make up?" Theia's gaze flits between us. "Oh my god, you two are well and truly fu—I mean, you're both glowing," she giggles with a smug grin.

"You're a pain in the ass, pup," Sam growls beside me and I can't help giggling at the siblings. I've never spent much time around them in the same room, but there's something so natural about them. The love I can feel radiating from the man by my side is enough to tell me how much he cares for his sister.

"I saw Kael yesterday," she says warily. "He's doing good."

The only response she gets is a huff from her brother. "Give my daughter here." He reaches out for our baby, and when his arms envelop her small frame my heart all but stops. The way she coos in his arms and then grips his shirt is enough to send my ovaries into overdrive for more babies.

"How is Kael?" I question.

"He's good, but he won't come here until the shit between him and Sam is sorted," she says quietly, but Sam doesn't answer, instead he stalks into the kitchen and leaves us staring at his retreating form. "Men," she huffs in frustration.

"What's that all about?"

"One day I'll tell you. Right now though, let's talk about you two." I join her on the sofa and can't help the grin on my face.

"We're getting married, well, kind of."

"What do you mean kind of?" She stares at me questioningly through narrowed eyes.

"He wants to collar me, like forever. He said he'd get me a ring too, so we'll be married, but…" I leave the sentence hanging when Sam saunters back into the living room carrying our daughter on his hip and three mugs in the other hand. When he sets them down, I notice they're filled with wine.

"It's a celebration. Figured we could all use a drink," he quips, handing them out to each of us.

"Yes, perfect. To you two finally getting it on." She lifts her mug and clinks it against mine, then meeting her brother's gaze questions, "How long has it been, Sam? You must have been one grumpy fucker without any." She giggles, then her big blue eyes widen as they settle on the little bundle of joy in Samael's arms. "I'm sorry, little Layla, but your father is known to be a really grumpy old man, hopefully with you around, he'll chill out a bit," she confides in her niece and a tiny gurgle, then giggle, escapes my baby.

"Theia, aren't you heading out?" The gruff complaint from Sam has me attempting to stifle a chuckle, but I can't hold it in. For the first time in too long, I'm laughing. A real, honest-to-God laugh.

Joy fills me as we settle into easy conversation about what Sam is going to do for a job, when Theia mentions that Dax may need help with the club. It seems our future isn't as dark as I once believed it would be.

Watching my family interact allows me to finally relax. To allow my emotions to catapult me into a feeling of safety and security. This is what I longed for. This is what I needed. After losing both parents and the life I once knew, I didn't think I'd see light again.

Even with Sam in the mansion, it felt as if every day was a battle. I suppose it was. I went to war beside him and we both made it out alive.

EPILOGUE
Samael

two years later

It's been two grueling years, but all the men who've ever hurt a girl, or woman are put away. Dax and I made sure that the place is completely shut down. Although some of the women have decided they'd like to turn it into a refuge. It will be gutted and rebuilt. My heart still hurts for all the girls I couldn't help, but those who got out are safe.

Closing my eyes, I remember the day it all clicked and I had to play the devoted son even though I wanted nothing more than to rip apart everything the empire stood for.

"Do you realize you'll turn out just like him?" my brother spits in my face. He's just been disowned, father's asked him to

leave and there's nothing I can do.

"Fuck you, Kael. Do you even know what you're giving up?" I turn to regard him with a ferocious glare. My little brother is not like me. He doesn't have the taste for blood. He's a Dom, a Master, but he doesn't enjoy the pain, the sadistic side that I do. Yes, I love marking pure flesh, but he likes the control, the utter devotion from a pet that allows him to feed and satiate that hunger that drives him.

On the other hand, when I see crimson seeping from beautiful smooth skin, it's my fuel. "Oh, make no mistake brother, I do," he bites back and turns to look at me. Dark pools of anger stab me. "I'm giving up the life of being the submissive bitch to the old man. Do you think he'll ever give his empire to you?"

"I'm not ready yet."

"You keep fucking telling yourself that. One day, when you realize what a fuck up you're turning into, don't come crawling to me. Because when you finally see him for the monster he is, that's when you'll open those pretty blue eyes and realize that this,"—he gestures around us—"isn't worth a fuck if you don't have love."

My brother, ever the romantic.

"Fuck love, and fuck you," I retort, but he doesn't waver.

"When you fall for a pet, a fuck toy, as you like to call them, then tell me those exact same words." With that, I watch Kael Wolfe walk out the door, out of the mansion, and away from the family legacy.

"Daddy! Daddy!" A loud screech drags me from the memory and paperwork I've been glued to for the last hour. Little blonde pigtails come bounding into my office and flop onto my lap. "Look!" The excitement on her face is enough to have me dropping everything to give her my full attention.

"What is that, my little poppet?" With a cute nose scrunch, Layla opens her hand and drops the beetle into my palm.

"A bug, ugh, bugs." She scrunches her face as she tells me earnestly that she doesn't like bugs and I can't help chuckling. She's only two years old, but she's started speaking easily, picking up words from Freya and me.

"But you've just been holding it in your hand, silly." She pulls herself onto my lap and sits up straight, but before she can continue her explanation, another shout comes from the hallway and I find Freya running after Mikael as he storms into the room gripping a beetle in his small fist.

"Da!" He shoves his hand at me which in turn has Layla screaming that there are bugs on her.

"Kids!" When Freya's in *mom mode* as I like to call it, I sit back and watch the fireworks. I still call her Angel, but that's reserved for our play time, which I think needs to happen really soon because I'm in the mood to show my wife how much I love her. "Sam!" Her shrill shout drags me from the images of her bound on my spanking bench and when I meet her glare she simmers down like the little kitten she is.

"You were saying?" Cocking my head to the side in question at her outburst, she blushes a beautiful shade of pink that I'd like to see on her ass.

"I'd like the kids to go to their aunt's tonight." It's as

if she's reading my mind, and I nod in agreement. "Great, I'll call Theia." Just then my Skype alerts me of a call. "Dax is calling now, we need to talk about work so I'll ask him." She nods, pulling the kids along with her and shutting my office door.

Hitting accept, I hear my partner's voice coming through the line. "Hey man, how you doing?" Since I finally got Angel back and she agreed to marry me, our lives have worked out and we've finally gotten our happily ever after. She's started her career as a dance teacher, and I've partnered up with Dax.

"Good, I've just finished the report for the new supplier. Did you get any more news about the building for the other club?" I ask as I pull up my email and hit send on the paperwork in question.

"Yeah, we can start renovations next week. We can head out there Saturday to check it out, but the space is big enough to have a floor and the bar in the shape you wanted." He confirms what I knew would happen. Since I was unemployed after Caged was shut down, I've been helping Dax with Inferno, and we've now expanded into other cities.

"Sounds good. I was about to call and see if you and pup would be able to watch the kids tonight?" As soon as the question is out, I hear my sister's giggle.

"Of course, you big lug. I'll be around in an hour to pick them up. They can stay the night. I'm sure you'll both need time to recover tomorrow as well," she informs me in that knowing tone. "Kael called. He's coming to visit with Paige next week," she adds before I can respond.

"Oh." It's been difficult with my brother back in my life. All I can do is hope we find the connection we so obviously lost all those years ago. "Thanks, I better go. See you later." Before she can respond, I hang up, not wanting to talk about my brother at that moment.

"What's the verdict?" I turn to regard my beautiful wife.

"Tonight I'm going to be doing filthy things to you, baby. I hope you're ready." Offering a wink, I revel in the blush that turns her cheeks a dick hardening shade of pink.

BONUS SCENE

Angel

Opening the laptop, I click on the files I've been too scared to look at for far too long. I've hidden the folder away, I've pushed it to the back of my mind, my life. It's the truth and I'm afraid of what it will tell me. I don't want to know what my parents went through when I was taken, but deep down, I know if I'm finally going to move on from my experience, I need to.

My therapist told me to face it head on. And even though I know Sam is here for me, fear has held me back from learning the truth. I'm only now coming to terms with the years of pain I endured. When I was a purchased toy for men to delve into their sick fantasies with.

I open the first document which is a video file. My father comes on screen and I immediately miss him. My heart aches as he settles himself in the familiar office chair.

"My name is Magnus Blythe, this is the confession

video of what happened in the disappearance of my daughter, Freya Blythe." He clears his throat, his eyes darting around the room as if he's afraid, but then continues. "I got involved with very bad people. Harlan and Harkin Wolfe are the men in charge of an elite club called Caged. It's a place my colleagues and I frequented. I never partook in any activities, but I've heard stories about what happens in the rooms."

I hit pause on the video because I'm not sure I want to hear more. Disgust lingers in my mouth and my throat burns with bile when I realize what my father is saying. I want to close the video, but I don't. I'm a masochist, so I hit play again.

"I've gotten into debt with Harlan, and as payment he's requested my daughter's life. When she turns sixteen, she'll be abducted, she'll be taken into Caged, and she'll work off the payment. I have no other choice but to let him take her. I don't have the money to pay him back, so I'm recording this video as evidence. Pumpkin, if you ever watch this, please forgive me. Please. I tried everything I could to get out of it, but it's done. Even if I fight him, he'll kill us all. Freya—" Glass crashes in the background, a scream I'm certain is my mother echoes through the speakers, then the screen goes black and a gunshot echoes through the the computer and hits directly into my heart.

"NO!! NO!!" My hand flies to my mouth in shock as I stare at the blank screen. There's more screaming, begging, and suddenly Samael's arms are around me.

"Baby, look at me, Angel!" His deep growl vibrates through me. Dragging my gaze from the screen, I meet his eyes that are filled with concern and agony.

"They… h-he s-sold me… they… he's dead." The pain that grips me is only second to what I felt when I lost Sam for those long months and when he tugs me into a tight hold I let it all out. All the pain, fear, and shame for what my father did tumbles from my eyes and I soak my husband's shirt.

His arms are warm and the calmness he exudes slowly seeps into me. "It's okay, baby, I'm here. I've got you. Cry as much as you need to, I'll always hold your pieces when you're falling apart, only to put you back together." His words soothe like a balm on a burn.

"I trusted him." My body is wracked with sobs as the emotion pours from me into him and all he does is absorb everything I give him. All these years I've lived with the belief that my parents were good people. But I believed a lie.

"Angel,"—strong hands cup my wet face and his gaze bores into mine—"you're my girl, you're strong and when you're not, I'm here, okay. Lean on me, cry on my shoulder, but don't ever let what you saw on that video make you love them any less. My father was a monster, yours didn't have a choice." I know he's trying to make me feel better, but I shake my head in disagreement.

"He did have a choice. I didn't." It's his turn to look at me in confusion. "As much as I hated where I ended up, and as much as I hated your father for everything he did, there's one thing that I gained out of all of this…out of this nightmare."

"What?"

"You." A small smile plays on his lips and he shakes his head.

"You've just seen a horrific video and you're here talking about me."

"Sam, you've given me a life. One that my father couldn't. Yes, he sent me into the wolf's lair, but I've come out with the beast himself." I confess, "I don't hate him, I don't think I ever could, but I'll never forgive him for what he did." He nods and pulls me into his arms again and let's me cry some more.

As he rocks me back and forth, he murmurs in my ear, "You know, baby, from the very start, from the moment I laid my eyes on you, I knew you'd give in to your desires. Since our first time, I knew my hunt was over because I realized you would fall prey to my darkness. From the very start, I knew you would be mine."

"And what if I fought you?" I question lazily once I'm all cried out.

"Then I would have waited forever at your door until you let me in. I am a gentleman you know, just a patient wolf lying low until the full moon appears."

"So I guess that makes me your moon," I suggest quietly, and he reaches for my collar, the one he bought for me two days after he asked me to marry him—a black and gunmetal tri-chain O ring choker with an angel wing hanging between my cleavage—and tugs on it.

"You are. You're my forever, Angel."

"And you are mine, Reaper."

The Reaper & His Angel

In you I've finally met my match,
I showed you my darkness,
and you were brave enough to love me anyway.
You are my moon, taming the beast within.
I am your wolf seeking peace.
You are my angel craving chaos.

Forever, Angel
Always, Reaper

If you loved Samael and Angel, meet Kael and Skyla next in the Forbidden Series. From the Ashes introduces us to Sam's brother, and we journey on a hot, steamy ride when he sees Skyla.

Are you ready for more Forbidden? Click here to meet Kael and Skyla!

Keep reading for an excerpt of From the Ashes…

PROLOGUE
Skyla

The lights are focused on us as we finish up our routine. The stages are in the center of a large lounge area and every man's eyes are glued to the two of us. We've become somewhat of a team. Men love my red hair and her chestnut locks. Her hazel eyes and my emerald pools seem to hypnotize them.

There are two platforms, mine which is off to the left has one sleek, silver pole, and to the right Dakota's has a chair, which she's currently leaning on as the song ends. Her long, slender legs shimmer with the glitter she brushed on earlier.

Inferno.

The nightclub that's given me a sanctuary from my past. An elite club with only the richest of clientele. They pay an exorbitant fee to see me wrap my legs around a metal pole. They watch me and the girls, sway and gyrate, wearing slinky outfits. They beg us to taunt them.

For the more exclusive clients, there's a menu if they'd like more than just a dance. When they request something from that sleek silver card, we're at their beck and call.

From where I'm positioned backstage, I notice Dax, my boss, and Axel, the head of security—the only two men I trust since leaving the hell I came from—stalking toward the bar. They've been good to me and the other girls who work for them.

"Skyla,"—Dakota's melodic voice drags me from my daydreams of another life—"orders up!" she quips, with a smile so bright it lights up her face. I know what she means, two clients requested us. The VIP package in this place means men can ask for any girl to join them in a private room, and if they pay the premium, they get to fuck us, and it seems tonight Kota—which is her stage name—and I will be entertaining someone.

I follow my best friend down the hallway. "Which room are we in?"

She glances at the card that Theia gave her and responds over her shoulder. "The Raven Room, looks like we have two men to dance for tonight." This room is mine—well, it's my favorite. With muted colors and a beautiful pole in the center, I feel as if they made it for me.

Upon entering we find the clients already seated in the onyx wingback chairs. They're both older, possibly mid-forties. One of them has a thick gold band on his ring finger, glimmering under the low lights coming from the ceiling.

"What can we do for you gentlemen today?" I stop only a few feet from them, my red panties and bra leave little to the imagination. Dakota heads to the pole, twirling around it hypnotically. I've been teaching her some moves and she's picking them up quickly.

"I'm Travis. This is Rich. He wants to watch, doesn't want

to cheat on his wife," the one with salt-and-pepper hair says, gesturing to his friend. I almost laugh at that. Of course he doesn't. "I, on the other hand, would love to control you and your little friend," he quips, and I nod in understanding.

"You want a dirty show?" I question, meeting the steel gray eyes of Rich. His dark brown hair is just graying at the sides. He nods. No fucking shame. "Fine, make yourselves comfortable."

Since I've been at Inferno, Dakota's one of the girls I've grown close to, the other is our hostess, Theia. They've both been an incredible support after the horrors I faced. They're both honest to a fault, and love me even in my self-loathing moments.

I think we do that for each other.

After my escape from Caged with the help of Dax, I've gotten attached to my makeshift family. Now, here in the Big Apple, a year into our friendship, we're like sisters.

Dakota's dressed in a skimpy, blue baby doll negligee, which is so short and see through, it's pretty pointless. She might as well be naked. She gives me that sexy little pout that drives her clients crazy. Raising my finger, I crook it to call her over. When I turn back to the men, I find both clients are now shirtless, and for older men, they're toned in all the right places.

Without a word, Dakota heads toward me. Her tits bounce with every step and their eyes are glued to her. "This here is Kota, boys, and I'm Skyla." Two sets of eyes flit between us with eagerness. "Kitten, why don't you show these gentlemen how sweet you can be."

I reach for her arm and tug her against me. My chest against her back. We're standing in front of Travis as I reach for her tits, groping them, tugging and tweaking her pebbled buds.

"Isn't she pretty boys?" Rich is fixated on our display. My

one hand travels down her flat stomach to find her bare little pussy. "Open your legs, K," she does and my fingers slip in easily. She's already wet and we've only just begun. I plunge two fingers into her, pumping them in and out. Her soft moans are the only sound in the room, until I hear the hiss of one zipper, then a second.

When I look at our audience, they've both got their dicks in their fists. Rich is smaller and not as thick, but the one who gets to play must easily be ten inches. That's going to hurt like a motherfucker. Pulling my fingers from her, I reach out to Travis. "Taste her," I murmur. He moves quickly, taking my fingers in his mouth and licking the sticky sweet juice from them.

"Fuck, that's delicious." He growls, then rises from the chair with his hungry gaze trained on us and shoves off the rest of his clothes. "I'm taking charge now. You're both going to lie down and obey." We don't argue because he doesn't look like he's joking.

His expression is something akin to someone who just hit the fucking jackpot. With two incredibly beautiful women doing as you wish, no man in his right mind could resist.

"Go sit on her face, pet. I think she needs to get a taste," he orders Dakota in a deep and rough tone. "Toys?" He turns to me, and I gesture to the chest of drawers. I know what he wants and he'll find them all in there. He pulls out the four thick leather cuffs and turns to the bed.

I lie back, watching him gawk as Kota's pert ass wiggles as she climbs on the bed. Rich is in awe staring at us as he strokes himself. She straddles my face and I immediately grip her hips, holding her against my mouth.

My tongue darts out, licking her smooth lips, tasting the

sweetness of her honey. The moans that escape her are feral and sexy. The sound of sex is in the air and the scent of K's sweet little cunt has me salivating.

"Enough." The word rumbles between us. Her eyes are glazed as she glares at Travis. I know she was close, wet and primed. "Lie down, sweetheart. We'll make you feel better." We swap positions, and he goes to work using the cuffs to bind her to the bed. Her legs are spread wide and her arms are locked in place. No escaping now, little one.

She watches me and I offer a wink.

"I need to come, please?" she begs, but he ignores her.

"Soon," I whisper. Her plump lips part with a moan when he tugs on her nipple. Grabbing the ten-inch dildo, he joins us on the bed, and in my peripheral, I notice Rich has moved closer.

"First we're going to devour you." Travis's tone is filled with need. He hands me the clamps and I nod. He doesn't need any motivation. Leaning in, he licks and sucks her sweet flesh.

Her nipples are peaks and I set to work laving and teasing them. Once I've got them both wet, I use the metal clamps—which are attached to a thin metal chain—securing them to each taut bud.

Her soft mewls are evidence that she's aching for her orgasm. I've learned over the year that she's very much a little masochist. She thrives on pain and this has put her in her element. "Oh, please, please?" she pleads, and I almost feel sorry for her, but he's in charge. He reaches for the third clamp from my hand—the one I haven't yet used—and stares at her pretty eyes.

"Now," he orders, and pinches her clit with the metal teeth. Her body convulses and Travis's face is soaked in her release. "Good girl, so fucking sweet." He murmurs and licks every *drop she's given him. His cock is rigid between his legs. With a quick glance at me, he commands in a deep tone, "I want you on her face while I fuck her." He grips his cock and I watch him rip the foil packet. "Sit on her face," he growls as he sheaths himself. I shift myself and straddle Dakota's pretty face. "Eat her cunt while I fuck you, little toy." I'm hovering over her mouth, and when her tongue darts out, it sends me spiraling. I grip the headboard and hold myself steady when I feel her sucking my hardened clit into her mouth. The pleasure shoots through my body, igniting my blood with a fire that races through my veins and I'm overcome with lust.*

Her body is shoved up every time he thrusts into her, which in turn has my body convulsing without thought and my release detonates, bursting through me as I cry out.

"What a beautiful fucking sight," he murmurs, in awe of me and my best friend. "Get off her face. We're both going to fuck her." On wobbly legs, I move off Kota, her face glistening with my arousal. He slips out of her and I help untie her. "I want you on your back." He points at me, then turns to her. "You, little doll, will ride that plastic cock while I own your tight ass." Rich is now standing at the bed. His body is tense as his hand moves slowly over his erection.

I lie back, donning the strap-on with Dakota on all fours over me. Her gasp as she sinks down on the dildo is a loud one. It's thick and I know it's filling her almost painfully. Pulling her over me, I watch her face contort as her puckered entrance is invaded by another solid intrusion. "Oh fuck, it's too much." Her whimper is soft and her eyes roll back in her head.

I latch on to her nipple, tugging the clamp with my teeth. I know the chain in turn tugs her clit and her body is now sandwiched between Travis and me. Suddenly, I feel the strap between my legs shifting and a dildo being teased into my pussy. Rich pushes it deeper. It's too much, too soon, when he starts fucking me with it.

We move in a rhythm that has fireworks shooting off behind my eyelids. My body convulses and spasms with the plastic cock inside me. When Travis hisses and spanks Dakota, her cries, his growl, and my own moans send me over and my orgasm grips me, sending me into outer-fucking-space.

AVAILABLE ON ALL E-RETAILERS

ACKNOWLEDGMENTS

With each book, and each one of these I have to write I still sit in awe of being able to hit publish. Sometimes I feel thank you's aren't enough because if I could, I send you each a hug and possibly you're own alpha male. Since that's impossible, I'll have to stick with this little message and hope it reaches you with all the love in the world because if it weren't for you, I wouldn't be here.

This couple, Samael and Angel came from a small idea and blossomed into an emotional story that had me writing at all hours of the day. They definitely will always hold a special place in my dark, little heart.

First and foremost to my incredible husband who puts up with my crazy writing schedule, he makes sure I eat, bathe, and have coffee when I'm on deadline. If it wasn't for him, I'm not sure I'd get through all the hours I put into each story. I love you babe. xx

Next, my BETA babes. You ladies are beyond incredible! Kenzie, Simmy, Lisa, Lizzie, Kate, Kristina, Becca, and Heather. If you didn't love Sam the first time I sent him to you in a sleepy stupor in October 2016, I'd probably have not found the courage to publish my first dark romance. Thank you ladies for giving Sam and Angel life.

To my editor Vanessa, and her team at PREMA for polishing this story to perfection. Thank you for your support, advice, and care you take with my work.

My Dreamers & Street Team, you ladies keep my sanity in check, it's not an easy job, so I have to thank you! For every share, post, repost, comment, review… It's your love and support that keep me going. So thank you, thank you, thank you!

The bloggers out there that have taken a chance on my work, thank you a million times over. Nothing can ever repay what you incredible ladies do for me, or any of us authors that you do so effortlessly and with such love. #AllBlogsMatter!

A special thank you to Lydia at HEA Book Tours & PR for assisting with this tour, you rock lady!! Thank you!!

And last, but definitely not least, to the readers, thank you so, so much for your support. For leaving reviews, for one clicking, for comments and posts. If it weren't for you, we wouldn't be doing what we love. Thank you! <3

If you want to keep up to date on all my books, hop on over to my read group on Facebook —> *Dani's Deviants*

Also by Dani

Head to my website for a full list of my incredible titles

www.danirene.com

About Dani

Dani is a *USA Today* Bestselling Author of seductive and deviant romance.

Her books range from the dark to emotional, but every hero is alpha, and each heroine is strong-willed, bringing the men down to their knees.

She now lives in the UK, after moving from Cape Town, with her better half who does all the cooking while she writes all the words.

When she's not writing, she can be found binge-watching the latest TV series, or working on graphic design. She has a healthy addiction to reading, tattoos, coffee, and ice cream.

www.danirene.com | info@danirene.com